PETE MILANO'S

Guide to Being a

MOVIE STAR

By TOMMY GREENWALD

Jack Strong Takes a Stand
Katie Friedman Gives Up Texting!
(And Lives to Tell About It.)
Pete Milano's Guide to Being a Movie Star

The CHARLIE JOE JACKSON Series

Charlie Joe Jackson's Guide to Not Reading
Charlie Joe Jackson's Guide to Extra Credit
Charlie Joe Jackson's Guide to Summer Vacation
Charlie Joe Jackson's Guide to Making Money
Charlie Joe Jackson's Guide to Planet Girl

Tommy Greenwald

PETE MILANO'S
Guide to Being a

MOVIE STAR

Illustrated by Rebecca Roher

Roaring Brook Press * New York

Text copyright © 2016 by Tommy Greenwald
Illustrations copyright © 2016 by Rebecca Roher
Inspired by illustrations drawn by J.P. Coovert for the Charlie Joe Jackson series
Published by Roaring Brook Press
Roaring Brook Press is a division of Holtzbrinck Publishing Holdings Limited Partnership
175 Fifth Avenue, New York, New York 10010
mackids.com

Library of Congress Cataloging-in-Publication Data

Names: Greenwald, Tommy.
Title: Pete Milano's guide to being a movie star / by Tommy Greenwald ; illustrations by Rebecca Roher.
Description: First edition. | New York : Roaring Brook Press, 2016. | Summary: Pete Milano, class clown,
    is used to getting into trouble while amusing people, but now his tricks have gained him an audition for
    a movie that could lead to stardom—and the loss of his girlfriend and other friends.
Identifiers: LCCN 2015026682| ISBN 9781626721678 (hardback) | ISBN 9781626721685 (ebook)
Subjects: | CYAC: Motion pictures—Production and direction—Fiction. | Middle schools—Fiction. |
    Schools—Fiction. | Friendship—Fiction. | Dating (Social customs)—Fiction. | Humorous stories. |
    BISAC: JUVENILE FICTION / Humorous Stories. | JUVENILE FICTION / Social Issues / Friendship.
Classification: LCC PZ7.G8523 Pet 2016 | DDC [Fic]—dc23
LC record available at http://lccn.loc.gov/2015026682

Our books may be purchased in bulk for promotional, educational, or business use. Please contact your
local bookseller or the Macmillan Corporate and Premium Sales Department at (800) 221-7945 ext.
5442 or by e-mail at MacmillanSpecialMarkets@macmillan.com.

First edition 2016
Book design by Andrew Arnold
Printed in the United States of America by R. R. Donnelley & Sons Company, Harrisonburg, Virginia

10 9 8 7 6 5 4 3 2 1

For the teachers.
And for the actual Pete Milano.
(No hard feelings.)

I tried not to make myself too handsome, but it's <u>not easy</u>!

INTRODUCTION

IT CAN'T BE THAT HARD to write a book, right?

I mean, if Charlie Joe Jackson can do it, *anyone* can do it.

So I thought I'd write a book about the time I became a movie star.

My book will be different from Charlie Joe's books, though.

For one thing, my book will have way more pictures, because I like to doodle a lot, and I'm better at drawing than I am at writing.

And also, I won't use as many fancy words as Charlie Joe does. He likes to show off his vocabulary. He's all like, "I don't like to read, but I'm so smart that I still know all these big words."

Well, so what. I don't know nearly as many big words as Charlie Joe, but last time I checked, he wasn't in a big Hollywood movie.

So there.

And I just want to say one other thing before we get going.

Everything that happened in this book happened because I'm kind of a troublemaker.

So I think the moral of the story is: If you get in trouble, interesting things will happen.

Act One
LIGHTS!

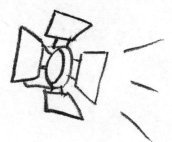

IT'S IMPOSSIBLE TO NOT
STEAL POM-POMS

"STOP HIM! STOP THAT BOY!"

That was Mrs. Collins yelling at me, as usual.

She yelled at me a lot because, for some reason, I do a lot of annoying things to her daughter, Eliza. I don't really know why I do them. I used to think it was because she

was so pretty and I knew she would never like someone like me, so I decided to make that decision easy for her by being a jerk. But then I got a girlfriend, and you would think that would make me less interested in annoying Eliza. But I was just as interested in annoying her as ever. Maybe because I knew she could take it. She has no problem sticking up for herself, that's for sure. And her mom has no problem sticking up for her, either.

STOP annoying my daughter just because she's beautiful and popular!

"STOP!" she yelled again.

But I didn't stop.

It's not like I planned it or anything. I'm not a big planner, like Charlie Joe. But when I walked by the cheerleaders on my way to soccer practice and I saw Eliza put her pom-poms on the grass, I was like, how can I *not* take them? Eliza wasn't even paying attention, since she was in the middle of one of those pyramid-formation things. And anyway, I knew I could outrun Eliza. But what I didn't realize was that Eliza's mom was there, too. She was probably sucking up to the coach, like all parents do. So anyway, Eliza is jumping around and not paying any attention, but the minute I grabbed those pompoms, I heard a scream: "Just what do you think you're doing?"

take ↓

also ← take

I looked up, saw Mrs. Collins staring down at me like an angry giraffe, and just took off.

I can easily outrun Mrs. Collins, I thought to myself.

But the only problem was that she got in her *car*.

I was pretty sure I couldn't outrun her car.

But I was sure going to try.

THE LADY WITH THE LAPTOPS

THE GOOD THING is that Eastport Middle School is really close to downtown, where there are a lot of little shops and streets and places to hide. And I knew that if I could just make it downtown, I had a much better chance of getting away.

I was halfway across the football field when I saw Mrs. Collins turn out of the school driveway in her fancy convertible. Her hair was flying in the wind like a magic carpet. She was driving fast. And in a school zone!

Where was Mr. Trenchler, the traffic warden, when you needed him?

I ditched the pom-poms in the bushes and took off down School Street, which is either a real coincidence, or named after the middle school. Anyway, Mrs. Collins was gaining on me—a car racing against a human isn't exactly a fair fight—so I ducked into the alley that leads to Harbor Street, which has a bunch of shops on one side and the river on the other. When she drove past the alley, she saw me and yelled, "Where did you put my daughter's pom-poms? They were very expensive, you little twerp!"

They didn't look that expensive at all, by the way.

I hollered back "In the bushes!" but she was already in the middle of making a U-turn. I realized she was about to head back toward me! So while her car was turned the other way I looked around for someplace to hide. The first place I saw was a fancy coffee shop called Just Brew It. I ran inside.

When I shut the door behind me, it was like the world disappeared. Everything got quiet. There were only three or four people in the store. All I could hear was someone breathing really loudly. After a minute I realized the person breathing was me.

"Hey, can I get you anything?"

I looked up to see a guy behind the counter. He was only a couple of years older than me, but he already had a ton of tattoos and earrings everywhere, including a bunch of places that weren't his ears.

"Ouch," I said, staring at a tiny metal hoop that went through his lip.

"Ouch yourself," said the guy.

"Oh, sorry, I didn't mean to say that out loud."

would YOU buy a latte from this guy?

The guy shrugged. "I've heard worse, plenty worse." He looked me up and down. "Aren't you a little young for coffee?"

"Oh, yeah, well I don't want anything," I said, my breath slowly returning to normal speed. "I was just running away from this crazy lady who was chasing me because I stole her daughter's pom-poms. But it's okay, because I threw them in the bushes."

"Ooookay," the guy said, shaking his head.

I was used to getting that reaction from people. The thing is, I have a problem with the truth—I always tell it. I can't help it. It's gotten me in real trouble. Lying is a lot safer, usually. I probably shouldn't be telling you that, but it's the truth. See, there I go again.

"Do you have a thing for pom-poms?" asked a voice behind me.

I turned around to see someone sitting at a table in the corner. I was pretty sure it was a woman, but I wasn't positive because she was hiding behind two laptops, and her face was smushed against a cell phone. She looked like a one-person Apple Store.

"Um, did you say something?"

The Apple-covered person hung up the phone. Yup—a lady, just like I thought.

"Yes, I just wondered if you had a thing for pom-poms. Why else would you steal them?"

Apparently, this is what BUSY looks like.

I scratched my head. This lady seemed kind of weird, but kind of funny.

"No, I don't have a thing for pom-poms," I said. "I just have a thing for getting on people's nerves sometimes."

"Why is that?" asked the lady.

"Because it makes life less boring, I guess."

She closed her two laptops—*click, click*—and looked up at me for the first time.

"I know exactly what you mean," she said.

RELATE-ABILITY

THE LADY WITH THE LAPTOPS turned out to be named Iris. She looked like she was about my mom's age, but I could tell she spent a lot more money on her hair than my mom did.

"Iris?" I said. "I've never heard that name before."

She sent a quick text or email from her phone, then looked up at me. "Well, my given name was Irene, but I changed it."

"Why?"

"It just wasn't getting the job done."

"What job?"

"The job of life."

I nodded, even though I had no idea what she was talking about.

She pointed to the chair next to her. "If you're going to hide out from the law, you may as well be comfortable about it. Take a seat."

"I'm not hiding out from the law," I pointed out. "Just someone's mom."

"Gotcha," said Iris.

I sat down.

Iris raised her hand to get the attention of the guy with all the earrings. "Can you please get my friend here a lemonade?"

"You got it," the guy said.

Iris looked at me so intensely that I felt kind of like an animal in the zoo—a weird, strange-looking animal, like an aardvark or something.

"What's your name, if you don't mind my asking?"

"Pete."

"So, Pete," Iris said. "Do you make a habit of causing trouble?"

"Maybe."

"Do you mind if I ask why?"

I thought for a second, trying to figure out why this Iris lady was asking me that. Maybe she was friends with Mrs. Collins! But probably not. Maybe she was one of those people that works in schools, dealing with the troublemakers, helping them get in touch with their feelings and all that.

But then that old tell-the-truth thing happened again, before I could stop it.

"'Causing trouble' sounds bad. It's more like I do things that I think are really funny, but sometimes it turns out that other people don't think they are nearly as funny as I do."

"I see," Iris said, nodding, still studying me.

"It's my turn to ask a question," I said.

Iris smiled. "Sure."

"Why are you asking me so many questions? I mean, I'm basically just a kid like any other kid."

"Well, that's just it," Iris said. "You have this thing that a lot of kids can relate to. 'Relate-ability' we call it in my business. The ability to relate."

"What business is that?"

Iris twirled a giant purple ring that was on her left pinkie.

"The movie business," she said.

Whoa.

"I love movies," I said.

"Me, too. That's why I picked this career."

"What do you do in the movie business?"

"I'm a producer," Iris said. "In fact, I'm here in Eastport looking at locations for a new project."

"Locations?"

"Places to shoot the movie," Iris explained.

I took a sip of my lemonade and tried to act like I'd met movie producers tons of times. But I hadn't, of course. Not even once, in fact.

"Cool," I said.

Iris was smiling. "So, Pete, I have one more question for you, if that would be okay."

"I got nowhere to be," I said, which made Iris laugh.

"Well," she said, "this might sound strange, but I'd like to have you read."

"Read what?"

She laughed again. "Sorry, I mean audition. For a part in the movie."

I coughed and a tiny bit of lemonade came out my nose. Then I said something that I think sounded kind of like "Blurghrwigegaa."

"I'm serious," she said. "We're having a tough time finding a kid to play a certain part, and you might be just what we're looking for."

I found my voice. "What? Seriously? What kind of kid?"

"Well, as it turns out," Iris said, "he's a little bit of a troublemaker."

"I can do that," I said.

"I bet you can," Iris said. Then she reached into her purse and pulled out a card, which she handed to me. IRIS GALT/PUDDING PRODUCTIONS, it said. LOS ANGELES, CALIFORNIA. "Go home and talk to your parents. If

Take my card!

they say okay, then call this number, and we'll go from there."

Her phone buzzed, and she looked at it. "Whoops," she said. Then she pushed a button and yelled, "Be right there, Sheldon!" It took her about five seconds to gather up her laptops, her phone, her purse, her bag, and her notebook and stand up. I swear, I've never seen anyone move that fast or carry that much stuff.

"Hope to see you again, Pete," she said, and flew out the door.

I waved, but she was long gone. Then I just sat there for a minute, trying to figure out what had just happened.

"Dude," said the tattooed, pierced guy. I jumped as if he'd woken me out of a deep sleep. "You want anything else?"

I shook my head. "Nah, I'm good."

I guess for once, I didn't tell the whole truth.

I was *better* than good.

HOME

THE FIRST THING I did when I left the coffee place was to get the pom-poms out of the bushes where I threw them, then bike over to Eliza's house and put them by the front door.

I didn't want to keep them, of course. What am I going to do with pom-poms? I just wanted to take them for a while.

Then I headed home. I wasn't sure anyone in my family would be there. But that's okay, because I knew they'd probably be right downstairs. The thing is, we live over my parents' restaurant—MILANO'S PIZZA AND PASTA. Everyone thinks it must be awesome living over your parents' restaurant, and it is sometimes. But the truth is, my dad is almost never home. He works all the time. And my mom works there, too, when my dad is shorthanded. Lately she'd been there a lot, because the restaurant wasn't doing that great. My dad says that people aren't eating out as much as they used to. I wouldn't really know about that, because we basically never eat out. And my dad owns a restaurant right downstairs! Where's the logic in that?

My Dad's office

I stepped into the restaurant and tried to get my parents' attention, but they were both busy with a little league team that had just come in to celebrate a big win. My mom saw me, though, and came over to give me a kiss.

"Ma, I have something to tell you!"

"I'll be up in an hour, Petey." My parents are the only people who are allowed to call me *Petey*, by the way, so don't get any ideas.

"Okay." As I headed upstairs, I could hear music, which meant my little sister Sylvia was home. She was probably doing homework. Sylvia is pretty much the exact opposite of me. Never gets in trouble. Never gets less than an A. And never, ever, ever was going to believe what I was about to tell her.

I knocked on her door and went in without waiting for an answer. "Hey, Syl, guess what?"

She looked up from her book.

"I'm going to be a movie star."

She rolled her eyes. "As if!"

Well, you can't just sit there and take it when your little sister talks to you like that.

So I went over, pushed her down on the bed, and started tickling her.

"Get off me!" she screamed, but she was giggling. I

wasn't hurting her or anything. I was just telling her who's boss. After about a minute, I let her go.

"You're such a big fat liar," Sylvia said, panting.

"Oh, yeah?" I reached into my pocket, pulled out Iris's business card, and threw it at my little sister.

"Pudding Productions?" she said. "What's that?"

"It's a company that makes movies," I explained. "This lady Iris works there, and she wants me to try out for the movie that they're shooting in Eastport."

"Shut up," Sylvia said, but before I could sit on her again, she screamed, "I take it back! I take it back!"

She scooted over to the side of the bed, and I told her the whole story: how I ran away from Mrs. Collins, how I ditched the pom-poms in the bushes, how I ducked into Just Brew It, how this lady started talking to me and examining me like I was a science project, and then telling me that she thought I should try out for her movie.

"So you're gonna be famous?" my sister asked. "Like, a movie star?"

"Nah," I said, but inside I was thinking, *Yeah*.

Sylvia pulled herself up off the bed and went to her desk. "If Mom and Dad let you," she said.

"What's that supposed to mean?"

"Well, they've been talking about having you work in the restaurant now that you're old enough, remember?"

Ugh. I did remember. "You need something to do after school," my mom would say, all the time. "You need an activity or else you're just going to keep getting in trouble all the time."

My dad would grunt in agreement. That was his main form of communication, unless he was mad. Then he would grunt really loudly, which meant it was time to sneak out of the room quietly.

I snatched the card back out of my sister's hand and put it away in a safe place. "Well, if I'm a movie star, that ought to keep me plenty busy."

"Did you text Mareli?"

I felt my face get hot. Mareli Quinones was my girlfriend. Well, kind of. Can someone be your girlfriend if you haven't kissed them yet? I hope so. I really liked

Mareli, but I was really shy about trying to kiss her. People would be surprised to hear that, because they think I'm the type of kid who's willing to try anything. But gluing your teacher's textbook closed is one thing. Kissing a girl is another.

"No, not yet," I answered.

"Why not?"

"Because I haven't, that's why." The truth was, I wasn't going to tell Mareli about the movie thing until I really believed it was true. And part of me didn't.

Mareli

Believe it or not, this girl actually likes me

Sylvia looked like she was going to make another smart-aleck comment, but she decided not to. Probably because she knew I would have grabbed her elbow skin and twisted it if she had. Have you ever grabbed someone's elbow skin? It's actually a good thing to do, because it hurts a little, but not a lot. So it's a good way to get a message across to someone, without causing any real damage.

Bella, our dog, started barking her head off. Which meant one of two things: Either we were about to get robbed by burglars, or Mom was home. I heard a key in the door. Most burglars don't have keys.

"Mom's home," I told my little sister.

"I hope she brought dinner," Syl said. "I'm starving." Remember earlier when I said we never eat out? Well, the good news was that we usually got whatever was on special at the restaurant, and it was *delicious*. (And I'm not just saying that.)

We both charged down the hall. Sylvia was ahead of me for the first three steps, until I shoved her aside and took the lead.

"Ow!" she howled. "You made me bang my head."

"Tell it to the judge," I said, which was a phrase I picked up from my dad, even though I had no idea what it meant.

When my mom opened the door, a lot of things happened at the same time: Bella jumped into my mom's arms, my sister smacked me on the butt, a pizza box went flying, and I yelled at the top of my lungs.

"MOM! YOU'LL NEVER BELIEVE IT! I'M GONNA BE A MOVIE STAR!"

My mom petted Bella and hugged Sylvia. Or maybe it was the other way around.

"That's terrific," she said. "But can we eat dinner first?"

HELLO? IS THIS HOLLYWOOD ON THE PHONE?

WHEN I TOLD MY MOM THE STORY, she interrupted me as soon as I got to the part about the pom-poms.

"Did you apologize to Eliza and her mother?"

"Not yet."

"Well, you need to call them."

"I will! Just let me finish the story!"

When I got to the part about the lady named Iris and me becoming a movie star, my mom interrupted again.

"Did this person offer you a part in the movie?"

"No," I said.

"Did she tell you about any other movies she's ever produced?"

"No," I said.

"Did you Google her company to make sure it was real?"

This time I just shook my head.

My mom let out one of those mom sighs. You know, the kind that says *Will these crazy kids ever learn?*

"Let me see the card," she said.

I ran to my room and got Iris's business card out of my shoe box where I keep all my valuable things, including the blue ribbon I won for drawing, my third grade report card where I got my first—and so far only—A, and the picture of my dad standing in a tub of shaving cream after I nailed the bull's-eye to dunk him at the school carnival.

I ran back to my mom. "See? It's real!"

"A business card doesn't make it real," my mom said.

"It has a pretty nice website," said my sister, who was sitting at the computer.

"Anyone can make a website," said my mom. She had an answer for everything.

I stared at her. "Well?"

She stared back. "Well what?"

"Are you gonna call?"

"You want me to call now?"

"Yes, I want you to call now! I need to set up my audition and stuff!"

My mom didn't move.

"MOM!" I yelled. Then, softer, I added, "She said I had relate-ability."

Sylvia was nodding. "Do it, Mom," she said.

I hugged my sister. "I take back everything bad I ever said about you, and every time I ever pinned your arms behind your back and sat on you until you couldn't breathe."

"Fine," my mom said, letting out another long sigh. "But if this turns out to be one of those fly-by-night companies that wants us to pay for ten weeks of acting lessons to get you ready for some audition for some big movie that doesn't actually exist, I'm going to send you kids to bed without any dessert."

"MOM!" my sister and I wailed.

"All right, all right," said my mom. "Get me my phone, it's in my purse."

"YAY!" my sister and I cheered.

Sylvia ran to get the phone, and we both watched as my mom dialed the number.

"Stop staring," said my mom. We stopped, for a second. Then we started staring again.

We heard a voice come on the line. "Hello," said my mom, "this is Anna Milano, Peter Milano's mother. Is this . . ."—she looked at the card—"Pudding Productions?" Then she whispered to us, "What kind of a name is Pudding Productions?"

"A delicious one," I whispered back.

"Yes?" my mom said, back into the phone. "Yes, I can hold, but only for a minute. I'm very busy." Then she whispered to us, "You can't let these people push you around."

"Definitely not," I whispered back.

We waited for about three minutes.

"Ugh," said my mom.

We waited two more minutes.

"I'm hanging up," said my mom.

"DON'T!" my sister and I wailed.

Finally, about thirty seconds later, I heard a voice come on the other end of the line.

"Hello? Yes, this is she," my mom said into the phone. She listened for about a minute. Then she said, "Oh, my, yes, of course I know who you are. Nice to speak with you, too." Then she listened for another thirty seconds, and said, "Yes." After fifteen more seconds, she said. "Absolutely, yes. Thank you very much." And she hung up the phone.

We waited for what seemed like twenty days, while my mom just sat there, not saying anything.

"WELL?" I hollered.

"YEAH, WELL?" Sylvia hollered.

My mom turned to me. "Do you know who that was on the phone?"

We stared at her, because we obviously didn't know.

"That was Sheldon Felden," she said.

"Who?"

"Sheldon Felden," my mom repeated. "One of the most famous producers in Hollywood. He's so famous even *I've* heard of him."

I felt my heart start to thump so loudly it practically drowned out everything around me.

"It turns out this woman Iris works for Mr. Felden," my

mom continued, "and they'd like you to go into New York City to audition for their new movie."

I don't really remember much of what happened right after that. I remember all of us screaming our heads off. I remember Sylvia jumping on top of me as I piggybacked her around the house, my mom calling my dad, and Bella diving under the couch because she had no idea what the heck was going on.

And I remember thinking to myself, *This can't really be happening. But it is!*

Only the third time in history
I willingly gave my sister a piggy back ride

REAL FRIENDS

BEFORE I DESCRIBE how everyone at school re-acted to the news about my maybe becoming a movie star, let me give you a little bit of background. It will help you understand everything that happened.

I go to Eastport Middle School, where most of the kids are from families a lot richer than mine. Which is fine, I guess. I don't really care, except when everyone gets all upset when they can't FaceTime me because I don't have an iPhone, or when people ask me what I did over Christ-mas vacation and then look at me funny when I say, "Stayed home." As if we would go away during one of the busiest times of the year for a restaurant! Anyway, that stuff is really annoying, but for the most part, people are okay.

My best friends at school are Timmy McGibney, Jake Katz, and Charlie Joe Jackson. But I'm not sure they would consider me *their* best friend, necessarily. Especially Charlie Joe. He's really pretty nice, I guess, but sometimes

I get the feeling he hangs around with me only when no one else is available. It's not his fault. I just think he likes some other kids a little more than me. Not that I blame him. If I were him, I'd probably feel the same way. I can be a little obnoxious sometimes.

But then, one day, everything changed. And it was all because of Mareli. She grew up in Puerto Rico and moved to Eastport last year. And she was the fanciest, most sophisticated, classiest, best-dressed person I'd ever met. So it made absolutely no sense that she decided to like me. I didn't believe it at first. I thought everyone was playing a joke on me when they started telling me that she liked me. You know why? Because it's the kind of joke *I* would have played on somebody.

Which is why, when Eliza Collins told me at lunch one day that she needed to talk to me, I expected bad news.

"You need to talk to me?" I asked her. "Seriously? About what?"

"Mareli."

And when she told me that it was true, that Mareli actually thought that underneath all my goofing-aroundness I was a nice, interesting person, I finally believed it myself. This girl actually *did* like me.

"And one other thing," Eliza told me. "Mareli saw the picture you drew of your dog, Millie."

Millie was the dog we had when I was younger. When she died I got really sad, and I missed her a lot, so I drew a picture of her for art class.

"Mareli thinks you have the soul of an artist," Eliza told me.

Art + Dogs = Girls liking you

"What does that mean?"

Eliza smiled at me. "I think it probably means you should ask her to be your girlfriend."

So I did. And she said yes. And from that point on, it didn't matter that I don't have an iPhone, or that I don't go to fancy islands on vacation like everyone else. I finally felt like a real part of the gang.

Then came the day I met Iris Galt.

As soon as I got to school the next day, I started telling people about auditioning for the movie. No one believed me.

Timmy McGibney was first. "You're auditioning for a movie? No way. You're lying."

"I never lie," I reminded him. It was a trait I was very proud of, even though it got me in trouble a lot.

Eric Cunkler chimed in next. Everyone kind of felt bad for Eric, since he had this rash on his neck that he couldn't seem to get rid of, but he was also super annoying, since he never had anything nice to say about anyone.

"There is absolutely no way that you will ever be in a professional movie," he said. "But if you want, I can take my phone and shoot a video of you sticking French fries up your nose, and we can put it on YouTube."

"Quiet, Eric," said Katie Friedman. Ah, Katie to the rescue, as usual. She was by far the most mature person in our grade. She'd straighten everything out. "So, Pete, are you sure this is a real thing and everything? Because it does seem a little strange that some random person would just ask you to be in a movie."

"Yeah, it does seem weird," Charlie Joe added, and then

everybody started putting in their two cents about what a loser I was that I could ever even think that I would be in a movie.

Thanks a lot, Katie Friedman.

"Quiet, all of you!" barked Mareli. She had a pretty sharp temper sometimes. It was one of the things I liked most about her. Except when it was directed at me.

Everybody got quiet.

"If Pete says he is auditioning for a movie, he is auditioning for a movie," Mareli announced. "The one thing we all know is that Pete doesn't lie. EVER."

Everyone murmured agreement at that.

"So tell us about this movie," Charlie Joe said. "What's it about? Who's in it? Why are they shooting it in Eastport?"

I hesitated before answering, because I knew it wasn't going to go well.

"I don't know, I don't know, and I have no idea," I said.

Everyone started howling.

"This is a joke," said Evan Franco, who was in all the school plays and considered himself the best actor in the school. "Sorry, Mareli, but your boyfriend here is full of it."

The bell rang for first period, and everyone started gathering up their stuff. I just stood there for a minute, trying to stay calm. These guys were supposed to be my *friends*; and yet here I was, with the most exciting news of my life, and everyone was basically treating it like a joke.

Except Mareli.

"Pete?" she said. "Can I tell you something?"

"What?" I said, without looking at her.

"My mom once told me something really interesting that I never forgot," Mareli said. "She said, everyone thinks that you can tell who your friends are when things are going badly. But the truth is, you can tell who your *real* friends are when things are going *well*."

I thought about that for a second, then decided I had no idea what Mareli was talking about.

"Huh?"

"When something great happens to somebody, people don't know how to react," she explained. "They get really jealous; they can't help it. So give these guys a little time. If they're really your friends, then they'll be happy for you, like I am. I promise."

"You really think so?"

"I know so."

And then she smiled at me, got up, and left.

I felt a lot better. Girls are like that.

When I got to my classroom, Timmy, Charlie Joe, and Jake Katz were waiting for me.

"Yo, sorry about before," Timmy said.

"It is really true?" Charlie Joe asked. "Are you going to be in a movie?"

"I'm going to *audition* for a movie," I explained again. "I probably won't even get it. I'll probably stink."

"No way, you'll be good," Jake said.

"We'll help you practice if you want," Timmy added.

Charlie Joe smacked me on the back. "Hollywood here we come!"

And then my friends and I decided that they'd come over after school and help me become the next Chris Pratt.

ACTING

WHEN WE ALL GOT TO MY HOUSE,

there was a package waiting for me on the kitchen table.

"What's this?" I asked my sister. Mom was downstairs at the restaurant, as usual.

Sylvia shrugged. "I have no idea, but it came special delivery."

Charlie Joe picked up the package and examined the label. "Pudding Productions," he said.

My heart started to pound. "Let me see that."

what's in this package could possibly change my life

I ripped the thing open and four pages fell out. Three typewritten pages were stapled together, and there was a separate, handwritten note. I read the note first, out loud.

Dear Pete:

Enclosed, please find the pages we'd like you to look at for your audition. This is a scene from the movie entitled Sammy and the Princess, to be produced by Sheldon Felden for Pudding Productions. You will be reading the part of Sammy.

Remember, Pete, the key is to be yourself. That is what we're looking for. That's why I wanted you to come in the first place!

We'll see you in New York next week.

Best,
Iris Galt
Executive Producer

P.S. Hope you returned the pom-poms.

"Sammy and the Princess?" said Timmy.

Charlie Joe snorted. "That sounds like a girly movie."

I was only half listening, because I was busy looking at the typewritten pages. It looked like it was a conversation between Sammy and some girl named Clarissa.

Then I had an idea.

"I need to practice this, you guys. Can one of you play this girl Clarissa?"

They looked at each other.

"I'll do it," Charlie Joe said.

"Cool."

"I'll film it," Jake said, getting out his phone. "That way we can analyze it later."

"What will we do?" Timmy and Sylvia whined.

I thought for a second. "Can you guys get us some Oreos?"

He grumbled, she grumbled, but off they went.

Charlie Joe and I went over to the kitchen table. I ripped out the staple and spread out the pages.

"What's the stuff at the top?" I asked.

"Stage directions," Charlie Joe said. "I recognize them from when I was in Mr. Twipple's play about the guy who invented paper towels."

"I remember that!" I said, howling. "You were scared to kiss Hannah!"

"Can we not talk about that?" Jake said, still filming us. Hannah was Jake's girlfriend, and he was supersensitive about her.

"Headmaster's office at a prep school," Charlie Joe read out loud. "Sammy is waiting for the headmaster to arrive. Suddenly the door bursts open and a girl rushes in.

She's the prettiest girl he's ever seen in his life. And she's crying."

Charlie Joe stopped, then looked at me. "Okay, dude, let's do this."

I closed my eyes for a second, and took a deep breath.

And then, for the first time in my life, I started acting.

SAMMY AND THE PRINCESS, SCENE 9

INT. HEADMASTER'S OFFICE AT A PREP SCHOOL—DAY

*SAMMY IS WAITING FOR THE HEADMASTER TO
ARRIVE . . . SUDDENLY THE DOOR BURSTS OPEN AND
A GIRL RUSHES IN. SHE'S THE PRETTIEST GIRL HE'S
EVER SEEN IN HIS LIFE. AND SHE'S CRYING.*

                    SAMMY
Whoa, whoa . . . Is everything okay?

                    GIRL (With a slight accent)
No . . . I mean . . . I . . . I do not
know.

                    SAMMY
Well, here, have a seat.

                    GIRL (Sitting)
This is so embarrassing. I do not cry.
If I was seen to be crying back home
in my country, it would be a national
embarrassment.

                    SAMMY
Wait, what?

                         GIRL
Nothing.

THEY SIT QUIETLY FOR A MINUTE

                         SAMMY
So, what are you in for?

                    GIRL (Not understanding)
                    I am sorry?

                         SAMMY
Did you do something wrong? If so, get
in line. I'm always the first one at
this party. My roommate loves to get
me in trouble. Today, for example, he
used my iPhone as a Ping-Pong paddle.
And of course, I got mad, so I threw
his charger in the toilet. And who's
the one that gets caught? Me, of
course!
      (He shows her a bruise on his arm)
Plus, I got smacked, just for fun.

                    GIRL
Oh my, that must hurt! No, I am not
in trouble. Of course I am not in
trouble.

                   SAMMY
Jeez . . . sorr-Y.

                    GIRL
I apologize. It's just that . . . I am
very far from home. It is my first day
here at school, and I am a bit lonely
and overwhelmed.

                   SAMMY
Oh . . . No, I get it. This place can
be tough on new kids. Heck, I was a
new kid once. Like, six weeks ago. I
hated it here.

                    GIRL
And now you like it?

                   SAMMY
No, I still hate it. But now I hate it
a little less. (He smiles at her) As
of two minutes ago.

THE GIRL LAUGHS AND BLUSHES

> GIRL
>
> That is very sweet of you.

> SAMMY
>
> Sweet's my middle name. But my first
> name's Sammy. And my last name is
> Powell.

THE GIRL LAUGHS AGAIN

> GIRL
>
> You are funny. Thank you for being
> funny.

> SAMMY
>
> Don't thank me. But you can tell me
> *your* name.

> GIRL
>
> My name is Clarissa.

> SAMMY
>
> Clarissa what?

THE GIRL HESITATES

SAMMY

What? Just Clarissa?

CLARISSA

I am sorry . . . but my complete name
is quite long.

SAMMY

Come on. How bad can it be?

CLARISSA

Very well. My full name is Clarissa de
Richemont Au Valle Excelsior Beau-
champs Les Filles Du Roi.

SAMMY

Wow. That *is* bad.

CLARISSA

Yes, very bad.

SAMMY

Do you mind if I ask what the heck
that all means?

CLARISSA

They are all the names of the royal
bloodlines of my family. And the last
few words mean "daughter of the king."

SAMMY (not believing his ears)
Daughter . . . of the . . .

CLARISSA

My father is Pierre X, King of
Malvania.

SAMMY

Making you . . .

CLARISSA

Princess Clarissa of Malvania.

SAMMY

Whoa.

CLARISSA

Yes. "Whoa." Whatever that means.

SAMMY

It means you probably aren't going to
want to be hanging around with the

likes of me very much. My roommate
Croft is probably going to be more
your speed.

CLARISSA GIVES HIM A LONG LOOK

                    CLARISSA
We shall see about it.

                    SAMMY
You mean, "We shall see about *that*?"

                    CLARISSA
Yes, Sammy. We shall see about *that*.

WHO'S THAT GIRL?

CHARLIE JOE AND I READ the whole scene about ten times before we both decided we were completely sick of it.

"Wow, you make a great princess," Jake told Charlie Joe.

"I can't wait for this movie to come out!" said my sister Sylvia. "Whether you're in it or not!"

Timmy picked up the script pages and started looking through them. "I want to meet Clarissa. I bet she's totally beautiful."

Jake laughed. "You know Clarissa's not a real person, right?"

"Of course I know that," Timmy said, not entirely convincingly.

"Anyone knows that," I added. "I bet Malvania doesn't even have a king."

"There is no Malvania," said Jake. "It's a made-up

country. The whole thing is made up. That's why they call it a movie."

"Oh," I said, embarrassed. I said dumb things like that all the time. I was kind of famous for it. But it wasn't because I was dumb, I swear. Sometimes I just say things without thinking. That's different than being dumb, right?

"Let's go play Xbox," Charlie Joe suggested. Nothing can change the subject better than Xbox.

Video games – the one thing boys can all agree on

But after we'd been playing for about five minutes, Jake said, "The girl who's playing Clarissa will have to be gorgeous."

The rest of us nodded in agreement.

"Maybe they'll ask Eliza to try out," suggested Timmy.

I suddenly had this weird uptight feeling. I was supposed to be the only kid from middle school who was asked to audition for the movie.

"You really think they might?" I asked, trying not to sound too against the idea.

Charlie Joe shook his head. "I doubt it. They don't just go around to schools looking for people to be in their movies." He smacked me on the back. "You're the only one, dude. You're it."

I quietly breathed a sigh of relief.

"Well, all I know is, she's gotta be superpretty," Timmy said. "Which is why she'll take one look at you and be like, 'Is this a joke'?"

Charlie Joe and Jake cackled and high-fived each other.

"Very funny," I said, but a part of me was thinking the same thing. I wasn't exactly considered movie-star handsome. Maybe she *would* think it was a joke!

I picked up the controller, started to play, and tried not to think about it.

But it was pretty much all I thought about for the next week.

THE BEST PART ABOUT
BEING IN A MOVIE

FIVE DAYS LATER, on a Wednesday, I was sitting in school when there was a knock on the door. One of the women who worked in the office came in and handed a note to Mrs. Albone, the teacher. Mrs. Albone looked up and gestured for me to come up to the front of the class.

"Good luck," whispered Katie Friedman, as I walked by.

"You'll do great," whispered Hannah Spivero.

"Say hi to Clarissa for me," whispered Charlie Joe.

"Don't forget your lines," whispered Evan Franco. "No wait, do."

I hope Evan Franco gets food poisoning from a fish stick.

After Mrs. Albone signed the note, I got my coat, headed down the hall, walked out of the school, and got into my mom's car.

In other words, I left school in the middle of English class to go to my audition.

Did you catch that? *In the middle of English class!* Man, it would be so great to be in a movie.

THE AUDITION

I SPENT THE WHOLE TRAIN RIDE into New York City studying my lines. I knew them by heart, but I studied them anyway. Mainly because I was too nervous to do anything else.

Nervous mom   Nervous-er kid

My mom came with me. She was already not in the greatest mood because she wasn't at the restaurant helping my dad. She was hoping we'd get to the production company office, do the audition in five minutes, be told thank you very much, and then be on our way.

So imagine her reaction when we walked through the door and saw about twenty other kids, all around my age, sitting there waiting their turns.

My mom marched up to the woman sitting at the desk. "Excuse me, can you tell me how long this is going to take?"

The woman looked up at her like she seriously couldn't be bothered. "Name, please."

My mom looked flustered. "Anna Milano."

"Child's name."

"Peter."

The woman flipped through some papers very, very, slowly. Finally she looked back up at my mom. "Shouldn't be more than a few hours."

"A FEW HOURS?" my mom exploded. "The letter said be here at 2:15!"

"Right," said the woman, as if that explained everything.

My mom spun around and stared at me. I was sure she was going to tell me we were leaving, so I started thinking about how I could get her to stay. But instead, she said, "I need to call your father." And she plopped down in a seat with a sigh.

Phew, I said to myself. *I still have a chance!*

I looked around and realized there were only boys. Where were all the girls? After a while, I noticed something else: The boys were getting called into another room one by one, but they weren't coming back out.

That spooked me out a little.

After about an hour, I went up to the woman at the desk. "Um, excuse me. Can you tell me where all the other kids are going?"

She didn't look up from the nail she was polishing. "They exit through another door, so they don't come back in here and talk about the audition in front of the other actors."

Actors?

"Oh," I said. "Thank you."

She looked up at me and finally decided to be nice. "You'll do fine," she said, actually kind of smiling. "Just try to relax."

"Okay."

Ha! Fat chance.

I closed my eyes and tried to clear my mind, but all that kept coming back was obnoxious Evan Franco telling me to forget my lines. So then I opened my eyes, but all that kept coming back was Evan Franco still telling me to forget my lines. So I tried to think happier thoughts, like what I was going to say to Evan when I got the part, how I was going to laugh in his face and tell him that I'd never invite him to the big movie premiere, and he would never get to meet any of the famous movie stars I became friends with, and how—

"Peter? Peter Milano?"

I jolted back to reality. My mom put down her book. There was a guy standing there. He had long hair, a clipboard, and a Sharpie.

"Uh, yes?"

The guy half nodded. "I'm Will. Come with me please." He looked at my mom. "This won't take longer than ten minutes. You can meet us in the outer lobby."

I got up, waited as my mom straightened out my collar, and followed the guy through the door into another room. It was huge. The back wall was made completely of mirrors, so I could see myself everywhere. That was superweird. At the front of the room there was a long table with about five people sitting behind it. Iris was smack in the middle.

"Pete!" she said, coming over to shake my hand. She turned back to the table. "This is the one I was telling

Scarf indoors, really?

Biggest glasses ever

you about, who stole the pom-poms," she said. The other people—two men and two women—all nodded, but none of them said anything. "Anyway, Pete, take a seat, and let's get started," Iris said. "Tell us a little bit about why you came in today."

Huh?

"Uh . . . because you told me to?"

The people at the table tittered.

"Lovely," said a guy who was wearing a big scarf, even though we were indoors and it wasn't cold. "But what makes you want to be an actor? Do you have a need to perform? To act out? To tell stories?"

This was totally not going the way I was expecting.

"Well . . . does acting out in class count?"

"Absolutely," said a woman whose eyeglasses were approximately the size of a small country.

"And I do tell a lot of stories. Usually as a way to try and get out of trouble. But since they're all true, I end up getting into more trouble than I would have in the first place."

No one said a word. They all just looked at me. Will, the guy who brought me into the audition, started heading to another door on the other side of the room, like he was getting ready to ask me to leave. Then I saw Iris whisper to the scarf guy, who shook his head. Iris whispered to him some more, and finally scarf guy nodded.

"Fine," he said. "Let's bring in S.F."

Iris winked at me, which I figured was a good sign. Then Will actually went to a *third* door—one that I hadn't noticed before, which was actually part of the mirrored wall—and opened it.

After about a minute, a girl walked out. I stared at her. I couldn't stop staring. I tried, but I couldn't. She was totally, totally, incredibly pretty—but it wasn't just that.

Will got a chair and put it right next to me. The girl came over and sat down. She couldn't have been more than twenty-five inches away. Possibly twenty-six.

"Hi," she said, with a smile that looked like ten toothpaste commercials rolled into one.

"Hi," I tried to say back, even though it probably sounded more like *Flughffff*.

She looked at the people behind the table. "He's kinda cute," she told them.

That gave me the confidence to

actually say a complete sentence. "Has anyone ever told you that you look a lot like Shana Fox?"

She laughed. "Yup. Probably because I *am* Shana Fox."

OMG.

Shana Fox, in case you've been living under a rock, is basically the most famous girl in America. She's been a big deal since practically before she was born. *Fox Rox!* is one of the most popular shows on TV. Plus, she's had like five hit songs. And she's been on pretty much every magazine cover ever invented.

Whoa, I thought to myself. *The last few weeks have been really weird, but things just went to a whole new level.*

"Okay, you two," Iris said. "Let's get to work."

I fumbled in my pockets, looking for the pages I'd studied, but immediately realized to my horror that I'd left them in the lobby. I tried to think of my lines but couldn't remember a word.

Freakin' Evan Franco, I thought to myself.

Sweat started forming above my eyebrows . . . but then a miracle happened.

"If you're looking for your pages, don't," said the scarf guy. "We're not going to be doing the scene."

I froze. "We're not?"

"Nope," he said. "We just want to talk, hang out, get a bit of a conversation going between you. Checking for chemistry, that sort of thing."

"Chemistry?" I said "Uh-oh. I'm not very good at science."

That got a big laugh out of everyone.

"Chemistry just means how you and Shana interact," Iris explained. "To see if you're good together."

"Oh, I get it," I said, completely not getting it.

But before I could think too much about it, Shana turned to me and asked, "So, do you have a girlfriend?"

"A girlfriend?"

She nodded, her giant eyes not blinking.

"Well, actually, I do," I said. "Her name's Mareli. She's pretty awesome. She's kind of out of my league, just between you and me." I thought for a second. "Actually, not just between you and me, since the whole school agrees."

Shana giggled. "I doubt that. You're adorable."

I think I turned redder than twenty fire trucks right then.

"I am?"

"Totally."

"Do you have a boyfriend?" I asked her. "I bet you have like a million boyfriends."

"Maybe," Shana said. "It's kind of hard, though."

"You mean, because you're like one of the most famous girls on the planet?"

"Well, I wasn't going to put it quite like that, but yeah, I guess so."

I was starting to feel my breathing return to human levels.

"What about Dex Bannion? Weren't you guys going out?" Dex Bannion was on her TV show. He was almost as pretty as she was.

Shana laughed out loud. "Don't believe everything you read on those stupid websites, Pete!"

The lady with the giant glasses suddenly piped up from behind the table. "Pete, I need to remind you that the confidentiality agreement you signed outside precludes you from discussing any aspects of this conversation with any form of media outlet, or even friends and family."

"Huh?" I said, confused.

Shana leaned over and whispered, "You're not allowed to talk about this conversation with anyone. You can't even tell anyone that you met me."

"Are you serious?" I said, louder than I meant to.

"Very," said glasses lady.

"But my friends are going to freak out when I tell them I hung out with Shana Fox!"

Shana put her hand on my arm. It kind of felt like she had shock buttons on her fingertips.

"Well, imagine how they'll feel if you tell them that we're making a movie together."

I felt a warm rush spread through my body. "Wait. Does that mean I got the part?"

"We'll call you," scarf guy said, which was Will's cue to steer me toward the door.

"Soon," Iris promised, shaking my hand as I was hustled by.

"It was nice to meet you, Pete," Shana called out.

"Bye, Shana!" I said, but there was no way she heard me, since the door was already closed.

ALMOST FAMOUS

THE NEXT DAY, I went to school and made my first mistake.

At recess, everyone crowded around me to ask about the audition. I told them about the room, and Will, and the guy with the scarf, and how nervous I was. By some miracle, I did manage to leave out the part about Shana Fox being the star of the movie and sitting twenty-six inches away from me and touching my arm with her electric fingertips. But everything else I said seemed to indicate that I was going to be a movie star any second.

"Did you find out who's playing your girlfriend?" Charlie Joe asked. "You know, the Princess of Wherever?"

"Malvania," Jake said.

"I don't know if she's my girlfriend in the movie," I said. "Just because of that one scene. Maybe she's somebody else's girlfriend back home in her country. We'll just have to see when I get to the set."

"The set?" asked Timmy.

"That's what they call where you make the movie," I told them. Lately I'd been Googling everything about the movie business. "Sometimes it's in a big studio with tons of lights and cameras and stuff, and sometimes it's on location, which means a real place, like a street or a house."

By now, a lot of other kids were crowding around and listening in.

"Where will your movie be made?" asked Phil Manning.

"Are you going to Hollywood?" asked his girlfriend, Celia Barbarossa.

"How much money will you make?"

"Will you meet anybody famous?"

"Are you going to quit school?"

"Are you even allowed to quit school?"

The questions just kept coming, and people were surrounding me, pushing in closer.

"That's enough!" shouted Mareli, barging through the crowd. "Leave him alone!" She was trying to get to me by pushing people out of the way. I guess she took the job of girlfriend pretty seriously.

By the time Mareli reached me, everyone else had backed up enough for her to look me right in the eye. "What's going on? Is this about the audition?"

"You bet," I said.

Mareli looked around. "Well, everyone seems to be

celebrating and congratulating you. So what happened? Tell us! Did you really get a part in a big Hollywood movie?"

I looked at her, and then stared out into the crowd of expectant faces.

"Yes," I said. "I got a part in a big Hollywood movie."

Noooooooooo!

You know how I told you earlier that I always told the truth, no matter what? I lied.

There's a first time for everything, right?

People immediately started congratulating me by grabbing me, pulling at me, and smacking me on my back and on my head.

"OW!" I said. "Easy!" But there was no stopping them. It was weird. They were treating me like a big star, and I hadn't even done anything yet. I always thought it was ridiculous when famous people complained about being famous. But all of a sudden, I kind of knew what they meant.

After a few minutes, I finally pulled myself out of the crowd and went into the bathroom to try and catch my breath by myself. Of course the door opened two seconds later, and Charlie Joe came in.

"Wow," he said. "You're really going to be in a movie. This is unbelievable. This is almost as crazy as when Hannah Spivero started going out with Jake Katz."

"This is actually crazier," I told Charlie Joe, but since

Hannah had broken his heart when she decided she liked Jake, there was no convincing him.

"They really told you you're going to be in the movie for sure? Right there at the audition?"

I looked down. "Yup."

"Amazing, dude," Charlie Joe said. "Congrats."

"Thanks."

Charlie Joe left, and I stared at myself in the mirror, thinking about what I'd just done.

So I told a small fib? So I left out the part about them saying they'd call me soon? So what? No big deal, right?

Wrong.

THE WAIT

BECAUSE THEY DIDN'T CALL

soon.

Or email soon.

Or phone or email *at all*.

Day after day, week after week, it was the same thing: I'd race home, sprint to the phone, check the messages, sprint to the computer, check the email, corner Sylvia and make sure she didn't erase an email by mistake, sit in my room trying to figure out how my life went so wrong, beg my parents to call Pudding Productions and find out what was taking so long, get in a big fight with my mom because she told me calling was a bad idea, and then try to figure out something else to do to take my mind off the whole nightmare.

At school, people kept asking me when I was going to begin shooting the movie.

"Soon," I'd say.

At soccer practice, my coach asked me if they'd figured out who was playing the princess yet.

"Any day now," I said.

And on and on.

Finally, after about a month, I couldn't take it anymore. I found Iris's business card and dialed the number. A girl who sounded about twelve years old answered the phone, "This is Pudding."

"Uh . . . hello, is Iris Galt there?"

"Who's calling?"

"Pete Milano."

"Hold please."

Five seconds . . . ten seconds . . . twenty seconds . . . forty seconds . . .

"Mr. Milano?" It was the twelve-year-old girl again.

"Yes?"

"I'm sorry, but Ms. Galt is in a meeting. Can I take a message?"

"When will she be out of the meeting? I'd really love to talk to her. I tried out for the movie *Sammy and the Princess* and they said they were going to call me soon but I haven't heard anything."

"I see. Well, as I'm sure you know, it's very, very

difficult to get a part in a movie. Many people auditioned. Have you checked with your agent?"

"I don't know what an agent is."

"I see. Okay, well I'm sure you'll be hearing something very soon. Good luck."

And she hung up.

I stared at the phone.

My sister stared at me. "What happened?" she asked. "Did you get the part?"

I wanted to yell at her. I wanted to scream, "YOU'RE SO ANNOYING! STOP ASKING ME THAT ALL THE TIME!!!" But I didn't. Because I knew that it wasn't her fault. But still, she was my  little sister, and sometimes little sisters are there just so you can get mad, when you need to get mad at *somebody*.

So I just said quietly, "What do you think? Does it look  like I got the part? Just leave me alone." And then I went to my room to think about how I was going to be able to deal with just being normal, non-movie-star Pete Milano again.

SF/10B

"I LIED!" I yelled one day at lunch, when I couldn't take it anymore.

Everyone stared at me.

"I lied," I repeated. "I didn't get the part. They never even called back. So you guys can stop asking me about it."

"But you never lie," Mareli said. "It's one of the things I like most about you."

"I guess I do now," I said.

By this point—a couple of months after the audition—I wanted to pretend like the whole thing had never happened. But kids kept asking me about it, and so finally, I blurted out the truth.

At first, people were kind of mad; but eventually, they just felt sorry for me. Everyone knew how embarrassed I was. So then, people started being almost extra nice. Fake nice. Even Ms. Ferrell, my guidance counselor who had told me about a thousand times over the years to straighten out my act, was going out of her way to be superfriendly. It was almost like people wanted the old, obnoxious Pete Milano back—but I wasn't quite ready to do that. I was still recovering from what seemed like a weird dream.

Things were finally, practically back to normal on the day that Timmy McGibney and I walked home after school, turned the corner, and saw a giant limousine parked in front of the restaurant.

Rich Person's car

Regular Person's car

My eyes jumped out of my head.

"Holy smokes," Timmy said. "What the heck is that?"

I didn't answer, because I was too busy running up the street, trying to control the pounding in my heart. Maybe the weird dream wasn't a weird dream after all. Now it was real life, and it was almost as if I knew exactly what was going to happen next.

I ran up to the car and stared at it. The license plate read, SF/10B.

SF = Shana Fox?

"No way," I whispered. "No way."

"No way what?" Timmy whined. "What's going on? Tell me!"

Could it actually be possible that Shana had come to my house in this crazy car to tell me herself? To ask me to be her costar? But what did 10B mean?

I sprinted upstairs, Timmy right behind me.

The first person I saw was my mom, standing in the kitchen.

"Is she here?" I gasped, out of breath. "Is Shana here?"

"Shana?" said my mom.

"Shana who?" said Timmy.

I burst into the kitchen and looked around. No Shana. But we did have a guest in our house. He was a little old man, wearing one of those really colorful Hawaiian shirts, a tiny little golfer's hat, and superwhite pants. He was sitting at the kitchen table having a cup of tea.

"Hello, young fella," the old guy said. "So sorry I'm not Shana. I completely understand your disappointment."

73

"Who are you?" I blurted out. "Is that your car? What does SF/10B stand for?"

"Shana who?" Timmy whispered. "Shana Fox? Are you guys talking about Shana Fox? Seriously?"

"Shush," I hissed.

The old man got up. I could hear his bones creak and crack as he stretched to his full height—which, believe it or not, was barely taller than me! But even though he was old, and short, and creaky, and dressed funny, there was something about his eyes. Something super intense. Something that said *power*.

"SF stands for my initials, and 10B stands for my world-wide gross."

We all stared at him, confused.

He laughed. "10 billion dollars, kid. Which is how much my movies have made around the world."

And suddenly I realized right away who he was.

"You're—"

"Sheldon Felden," he said. "Happy to know ya."

He stuck out a wrinkled hand, and I shook it. His hyper-powerful eyes twinkled.

"Welcome to the movies."

The moment my life changed forever

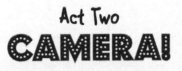

Act Two
CAMERA!

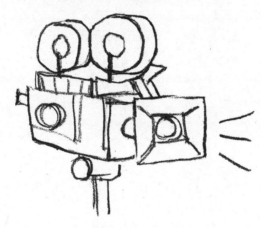

SAMMY AND THE PRINCESS, SCENE 1

FADE IN:

*EXT. IN FRONT OF A DORM AT A BOARDING SCHOOL—
DAY*

*THE MOVIE OPENS AS SAMMY POWELL, AROUND
14 YEARS OLD, IS GETTING OUT OF THE CAR, READY
FOR HIS FIRST DAY AT A PRIVATE BOARDING SCHOOL.
IT'S A FANCY SCHOOL, WHICH MAKES SAMMY, WHOSE
FAMILY ISN'T RICH, A LITTLE NERVOUS. SAMMY'S
PARENTS ARE UNLOADING THE CAR.*

> DAD
>
> Sammy, a little help here?

> SAMMY (Staring at the other kids)
> In a minute, Dad.

> MOM
>
> Sammy, I know you're nervous . . .
> jeez, I'd be nervous too if I were you.
> But this place is truly amazing. Just
> the fact that you're able to go
> here . . . and get a scholarship . . .
> we're just so proud of you, honey.

                    SAMMY

I miss my friends. These kids
look . . . weird.

                    DAD

Don't be ridiculous. They look smart!
Ready for success!

                    SAMMY

Whatever. (Gets a text) Grandma wants
to know what the kids are like. (He
types) "Preppie heaven, Grandma."

JUST THEN, A COUPLE OF KIDS WALK UP TO THE CAR

               KID 1 (To Sammy)
What kind of car is that?

                    SAMMY

Uh, . . . it's like a Dodge or something, I guess.

                    KID 2

Man, I didn't know they let cars like
that in this place.

                    SAMMY
    Huh?

BUT THE KIDS SNICKER AND RUN AWAY

                    MOM
    What was that about, honey?

                    SAMMY
    Oh, nothing.

BY NOW THE CAR IS COMPLETELY UNPACKED

                    DAD
    Ready to head inside, son?

IT'S THE LAST THING SAMMY IS READY FOR

                    SAMMY (Sarcastic)
    Can't wait, Dad. Cannot WAIT.

THE NIGHT BEFORE

SUNDAY NIGHTS ARE ALWAYS packed at Milano's Pizza and Pasta. My dad says it's because by the end of the weekend, parents are tired of running around with their kids and they just want to go out and relax and not have to worry about things like cooking and cleaning up.

The funny thing is, we NEVER eat out as a family on Sunday nights. Because my parents are too busy feeding everyone else.

But this Sunday was different. It was the night before my first day working on the movie, and my parents decided it was time to celebrate with a big dinner at the corner table. They said I could bring three friends, too, so I brought Mareli, Charlie Joe, and Timmy. My sister Sylvia was there, too, being embarrassing as usual.

"My parents own this restaurant," she said to anyone who would listen.

Even though it was supposed to be a big family

celebration, Mom and Dad were working pretty much the whole time. They were happiest when they were running around like maniacs. I guess you kind of have to be like that if you want to be in the restaurant business.

"I want to make a toast," said my dad, during one of the few times he was actually sitting at the table. "To my son, the actor. I always knew he had the kind of personality that would get him noticed one day. I just thought it would be by the police, not some hotshot Hollywood movie producer." We all laughed. My dad raised his glass of beer, and we all raised our glasses of root beer. "So here's to Petey. May he become such a big success, that

one day I never have to make another pineapple and hummus pizza." My dad shook his head. He was an old-fashioned guy, and he always had a hard time with the crazy stuff people were putting on pizza these days.

Everybody cheered, "To Pete!" except Charlie Joe, who cheered, "To Petey!"

"Don't you dare," I told him.

My friends had begged me to bring the script to dinner, but Mr. Felden had told me I wasn't allowed to show it to anyone. I brought the first couple of pages anyway.

"Let's read it out loud," Charlie Joe suggested.

"Awesome idea," Timmy added.

Charlie Joe winked. "I want to see the magic. The Milano magic."

"Cut it out you guys," I said. Secretly I was worried: What if there *is* no magic?

"Come ON," Sylvia whined, and at that point I knew there was no way out of it.

So we did the scene. My parents pretended to be Sammy's parents, which was kind of weird. The annoying kids were played by Charlie Joe and Timmy. Sylvia whined that there was no part for her, so I let her read the directions.

When I got to the line that said, "Preppie heaven, Grandma," everyone laughed, as if I actually knew what I was doing. Which was a good thing, since I was totally freaked out that I had NO idea what I was doing, and when I got to the movie set, everyone was going to realize they'd made a horrible mistake.

When I said the last line—"Cannot WAIT"—everybody started clapping.

"All right!" Charlie Joe said. "Hollywood look out! Here comes Petey Milano!"

I shot him a look.

But when Mareli hugged me, I thought for the first time that maybe I could actually pull this off.

Then she pulled out a small package. "We got you something."

"Are you guys kidding?" I said. "You totally didn't have to do this."

Mareli blushed. "We wanted to."

"Awesome, thanks." I ripped open the package—inside was the coolest pair of sunglasses I'd ever seen in my life.

I couldn't believe it.

"Whoa," I said. "These are supersweet."

"You kids are wonderful," my mom said, her smile a mile wide.

"Thanks everyone," I said. "I mean, seriously. Thanks so much. You guys are the best."

"It was Mareli's idea," Charlie Joe said.

I looked at her. "Seriously?" But she was looking at the ground, smiling.

Timmy grabbed them out of my hand and put them on. "Yo, maybe I should be an actor!"

"Dude, every movie star has a sweet pair of shades," Charlie Joe told me. "It's part of the deal."

"Nah," I said, "I'm just a doofus who walked into the right coffee shop. I got lucky, that's it. For real."

"You're not just a doofus, and you didn't just get lucky," my dad said. "You're talented. I can tell just from how you read that short scene. You'll be fantastic."

"Thanks, Dad," I said, feeling warm inside. There's something about when your dad says something nice about you—I don't know what it is, but it's the best feeling in the world.

Mareli took the sunglasses from Timmy and handed them to me. "Try them on."

"This is crazy," I said. But I put them on. Then I looked at my reflection in the window.

And you know what?

I looked good.

Now it's official.

MRS. SLEEP

"SO, MR. MILANO, are you ready to become Eastport Middle School's first movie star?"

Mrs. Sleep stared down at me, and I shifted in my seat. That's what kids do when they're in the principal's office, right? They shift in their seats.

For once, though, I wasn't in the principal's office for something I did wrong, like throwing a Frisbee at Eliza Collins's butt or trying to drink from the water fountain with a straw.

Nope. I was there for something I did *right*. I got a part in a movie! Now Mrs. Sleep wanted to make sure it wouldn't disrupt my schoolwork.

"Are you?" she repeated.

"I guess so, Mrs. Sleep," I answered nervously. She was the one person in the world who actually scared me a little bit.

"You mean you *know* so," said Ms. Ferrell, my guidance counselor, who was there, too.

"Right. I know so."

Mrs. Sleep adjusted her glasses, which were so thick and magnified her eyes looked like an alien's. "Excellent. Well, I have some more good news. Because of the unusual circumstances of this situation, I'm going to grant you a unique opportunity."

The Principal's Office
(also known as "the worst place on earth")

My mom was sitting behind me, and I could hear her shifting in *her* seat. That's how scary Mrs. Sleep was—she could even make *adults* shift in their seats!

"A unique opportunity?" I said.

"Indeed." A fly buzzed around the room, and Mrs. Sleep swatted at it. I think she got it, too. "Mr. Milano, as you are unable to complete your class attendance requirements because of this film shoot, you will be taking on a special project all your own."

Uh-oh. I didn't like the sound of that. "What kind of project?"

"I'm pleased to tell you that once your work on the film is completed, you will be asked to write a special paper on the experience, which will be presented to myself and Ms. Ferrell, as well as your language arts teacher, Mrs. Albone."

"A special paper?" I sputtered. "How special?"

Mrs. Sleep stood up and rose to her full height, which seemed about twice as tall as my dad. "I'd say about ten pages special," she said. "Congratulations again!"

After the meeting, we were halfway down the hall before my mom worked up the nerve to speak. "Jeez, I'm impressed," she whispered.

"Huh? With what?"

She shook her head. "With the fact that you've been able to survive so many visits to that office," she said.

JUST NANO

THE FIRST THING YOU NOTICE when you walk on to a movie set is the food.

It's everywhere.

The movie set
also known as "the _best_ place on earth"

There's junk food; health food; hot food; cold food; fruit, sweets, nuts, and berries; every kind of drink you could possibly imagine; and a guy whose only job is to make omelets.

And it's all free.

It's almost like a bar mitzvah, only instead of a bunch of hyper kids running around hopped up on candy and soda, you've got a bunch of hyper adults running around with headphones on, yelling things that don't make any sense.

"We need the grip on set!"

"Ten minutes to talent!"

"Last looks!"

"Back to one!"

My mom and I were told to wait inside a big trailer that was just outside the studio. Inside the trailer there was a fruit-and-cookie basket about a mile high. My mom inspected the goods.

"Fresh," she said, nodding her head in approval.

There was a knock on the door, and a totally pretty young woman came bouncing in like she was on a pogo stick.

"Hi!" she said. "I'm Ashley Kinsley! I'm going to be Pete's wrangler. I'll be the one making sure he doesn't work overtime or anything like that. Very strict child labor laws in this state, you know!"

"Wrangler?" my mom asked, popping a piece of mango in her mouth. "That sounds like an interesting job."

"It is," Ashley said. "But mainly, it's a way to get my foot in the door. I'm going to be a director."

"Well, hopefully that will work out for you," said my mom.

Ashley nodded like a bobblehead. "Oh, it will," she said. "I have no doubt."

I was starting to learn that the one thing you had to have in the movie business was confidence.

Ashley turned her really blue eyes to me. "So, Pete! We need to take a walk. You ready?"

My mom got up first. "Well, guess I'll hit the road." She looked at Ashley. "What time should I pick him up?"

Ashley giggled. "Oh, we just needed you here today to fill out some paperwork," she explained. "But in general, we'll have a car pick him up and take him home every day."

"Excuse me?" said my mom.

"A car will take Pete to work every day. It's standard."

My mom shook her head and looked at me. "Well, Petey, my little star," she said. "I've barely ever been in a taxi." But she winked and gave me a big hug. "Text me all day long," she said.

"I will," I promised.

"Actually, we try to discourage phones on the set." Ashley said.

"Good idea," said my mom. "Except text me anyway."

Ashley and I headed out of the trailer and weaved our way through what seemed like a small army of people, all carrying stuff, shouting stuff, and eating and drinking stuff. Finally, after about five minutes, we were standing in front of a small building that looked like a miniature White House.

"What's in there?" I asked Ashley.

"The man," she answered.

"Which man?" I said, but by then we were through the door and into an office filled with huge piles of paper. HUGE piles of paper.

"Scripts," Ashley said, answering my unasked question. "Everyone wants to make a movie with Sheldon."

"That's right, they do," croaked a voice, and I turned around to see Sheldon Felden walking slowly into the room. He was using a cane, which looked like it was carved out of the nicest wood that came off the nicest tree that grew in the nicest forest in the world. In other words, that was one sweet cane.

Behind Mr. Felden were two people: a huge football-player-type guy who was probably like a bodyguard or something, and the guy with the scarf who'd been at the audition.

"Hello, son," Mr. Felden said, shaking my hand. He had a really strong grip for an old man.

"Nice to see you again, sir," I told him. "I'm really excited to be here."

"Well, that's swell, we're excited that you're here." He turned around. "You remember Nano?"

The scarf guy stepped forward. He didn't look all that happy to see me. "Hello, Pete, nice to see you again. I'm Nano, the director of the film."

"Oh, hey, Mr. Nano."

He shook his head, the scarf flopping back and forth. "It's just Nano."

"Oh. Sorry. Well, it's an honor to be here, Nano."

Mr. Felden sat down behind his desk with a big sigh. "Pete, I'm going to be straight with you," he said. "There are some people who didn't particularly want you for this picture."

"Picture?" I asked.

"That's what older people call movies," Ashley whispered.

"They didn't want you because you're a little young, and you don't have any experience," Mr. Felden said. "And they're right. You don't."

I had a feeling Mr. Nano—I mean Nano—was one of those people. I looked at him, but he refused to take his eyes off Mr. Felden, who wasn't finished talking.

"But Iris thought you had something, and she was pushing for you. And when I took a look at your audition tape, I had to agree with her. So we're going out on a limb for you here, Pete. You're not going to make me look bad, are you?"

"No, sir," I said. "Definitely not."

"Good! Now, Nano, tell Pete a little bit about the part."

Nano sat down, took out his iPad, and said, "Let's chat a bit about who Sammy really is." Then he talked for about twenty minutes straight. I'm not even sure he took a breath. Mr. Felden's no dummy, though: after the first ten seconds, he grabbed his cane. "See you kids later," he wheezed, then he got the heck out of there.

I tried to listen to Nano, I really did, but it was hard. I've never been a great listener—not to my parents, not to my teachers. It's just something I'm not good at. But this was important—*really* important—so I tried hard to concentrate. The problem was, he had this mole underneath his bottom lip that kind of jumped around when he talked. It was amazing and fascinating and very distracting.

This is my listening face.

Finally, Nano stopped. "Any questions? About the movie in general, or Sammy's character motivations?"

I froze. Was there going to be a test?

"Uh, no sir, Mr. Nano."

"Just Nano."

"Nano."

He jumped up. "Good. Ashley, take him to wardrobe. Let's go make a movie."

"What's wardrobe?" I asked Ashley.

She laughed. "It's where you stop being Pete Milano and start being Sammy Powell."

FIRST RULE OF SHOW BUSINESS

AFTER I GOT MY SIZES taken for Sammy's main outfit—basically a prep school uniform, shirt, tie, and khaki pants—Ashley brought me into a giant room that looked like it could fit two airplanes inside, easy. But it was completely empty, except for one long table and a bunch of chairs.

"This is the soundstage, where a lot of the shooting will take place," she explained. "Today, though, we're just doing a table read to get started."

I was already self-conscious about the fact that I didn't know anything about anything, but I asked anyway. "What's a table read?"

"It's where all the actors sit around the table and just read the script all the way through," she explained. "It's a great way for everyone to get to know each other, and just see how the story flows."

I heard voices behind me and realized that the room was slowly filling up with people.

"Is Iris around?" I asked, hoping for a familiar face.

"No, she's back in L.A.," Ashley said. "Hopefully she'll come to the set when we shoot the locations up in East-port."

"When is that?"

"At the very end of the shoot." Ashley didn't seem at all bothered by the fact that I'd asked her about sixty-two questions in less than an hour.

As the new people got closer, I realized some of them were actually not unfamiliar at all. In fact, some of them were completely and totally familiar.

Because they were famous.

The first person I recognized was Adam Blankman, who'd been in some hilarious movies, including *Cop Dog* and *Walking On Milk*. Next to him was Becky Sue Wood-cock, a country singer who'd won *Sing It America!* a few years back.

"Holy moly," I said to myself. Only, I guess it wasn't to-tally to myself, because Ashley looked up from her phone.

"Oh, cool," she said, "the other actors are here. Come say hi."

We walked over, and I could feel all eyes turn to me, as people said to themselves, *Who's this rookie?* It reminded me of Mareli's first day in school after she'd moved here from Puerto Rico, and she was sitting by herself at lunch, and for some reason I decided to go up to her, grab five of her French fries, and eat them. She looked up and said,

"You're the rudest person I've ever met." Who knows? Maybe that's the moment she decided to like me.

"Everyone, this is Pete Milano," Ashley said. "Our Sammy Powell."

Mr. Blankman smiled and shook my hand. "Cool! Welcome aboard. I'm playing your pops. I bow down to you, because you have about three thousand more lines than me."

"Wow," I said, because I couldn't think of anything else to say.

Ms. Woodcock gave me a big hug. "And I'm your mom, so don't try any funny stuff, young fella." She had a thick Southern accent, a really short skirt, and the biggest head of red hair I'd ever seen. It was kind of hard to imagine her as *anyone's* mother.

My movie parents (slightly better looking than my real parents)

I got introduced to a bunch of other people, some who were playing other, smaller parts, and some people who were producers and behind-the-scenes people, and then we all just kind of stood around, like we were waiting for something to happen.

As it turned out, we were waiting for some*one* to happen.

About ten minutes later, I saw a few people start whispering into their walkie-talkies (a lot of people have walkie-talkies on movie sets), and then all of a sudden five people walked into the room really fast, talking or texting on their cell phones.

Thirty seconds after that, a golf cart came whizzing through the door. I couldn't tell who was driving, but in the passenger seat was Shana Fox.

"Hi, everyone! So sorry I'm late!" She hopped out and started air-kissing everyone in the room. I waited for her to get to me and thought about what I'd say to her. She'd been so nice when we met at my audition. But when she shook my hand, she looked as if she'd never seen me before.

"Remember Pete?" Ashley asked her. "He's playing Sammy."

Shana squinted her eyes. "Oh, yes, right!" she said. "I apologize. We looked at so many boys for that part." (*We??*) She shook my hand. "Well, congratulations, Pete. I look forward to working with you." And then she was on to the next person.

Ashley watched me watch her go. "When she's on set,

she's a different person," she explained. "All business. It's like she's a thirty-four-year-old actress in a fifteen-year-old's body."

"She's fifteen already?" I asked.

"Yup," Ashley laughed. "And that's as old as she's gonna get for about ten years, if her managers have anything to say about it."

The guy who was driving the golf cart walked over to us, and I realized it was Dex Bannion, the guy from Shana's TV show who Shana said wasn't her boyfriend.

"Yo," he said, pumping my hand. "I'm Dex."

"I'm Pete," I said. "Nice to meet you."

He punched Ashley in the arm. "Yo, girl, wassup?"

"Easy on the yo," Ashley told him. "And also, aren't you a little young to be driving a golf cart?"

"I'm sixteen, yo," he answered.

Ashley turned to me. "Dex is going to be playing Croft."

Whoa. Things just got a lot more intense.

"Your nemesis," Dex added, with a nemesis-like smile.

Every movie needs a bad guy

"Wow," I said. "Cool. That's great."

He shook his head. "Nah, not that cool, to be honest with you. It's a jive movie, and I got bigger fish to fry, bro. But I'm doin' it as a favor to my lady."

"Your lady?"

He nodded in the direction of Shana. "Right there, bro."

I was confused. "But—"

"It looks like Nano is about to get started," Ashley said, cutting me off.

Dex nodded. "Aaaiite," he said. "Peace."

Ashley and I watched as Dex hopped in his golf cart and weaved his way to the table, annoying a bunch of people in the process. "At my audition, Shana told me they weren't going out," I said.

Ashley looked at me like I was two years old.

"First rule of show business, Pete," she said. "Never believe a word anyone says."

SAMMY AND THE PRINCESS, SCENE 4

INT. DORM ROOM—NIGHT

SAMMY IS UNPACKING IN HIS ROOM WHEN A MAN WALKS IN, CARRYING FIVE SUITCASES. HE PUTS THEM DOWN, HUFFING AND PUFFING. THEN HE EXITS. A MINUTE LATER, A KID WALKS IN.

> KID (calling off to the man)
> Much obliged, Perkins.

THE KID'S NAME IS CROFT CHANDLER, AND HE LOOKS LIKE HE OWNS THE PLACE. WHICH, GIVEN WHO HIS FAMILY IS, ISN'T FAR FROM THE TRUTH. CROFT NOTICES SAMMY.

> CROFT
> Yo, you must be . . .

> SAMMY
> Sammy. Sammy Powell.

> CROFT
> Right, Sammy.

SAMMY WAITS FOR THE KID TO INTRODUCE HIMSELF.
HE DOESN'T.

                    SAMMY
And you are . . . ?

                    CROFT
Oh, right. Where are my manners? Croft
Chandler.

                    SAMMY
Croft Chandler?

                    CROFT
That's right.

                    SAMMY
Uh . . . which one is your first name?

                    CROFT
Is that a joke?

                    SAMMY
Actually, no.

                    CROFT
Don't you know who I am?

                    SAMMY
Actually, no again.

                    CROFT
Come here, let me show you something.

CROFT GUIDES SAMMY OVER TO THE WINDOW

                    CROFT
See that building, across the quad?
That's the Chandler library right
there.

                    SAMMY
As in Croft Chandler?

                    CROFT
That's the one. So just a tip, kid: you
might want to get a handle on the
traditions around here, and the people
who matter. It will go a long way. Now
go get me a coffee.

                    SAMMY
Huh?

                    CROFT

A coffee. Light with milk.

                    SAMMY

You drink coffee?

                    CROFT

D'uh.

                    SAMMY

Okay, well, that's weird. And, what's
also weird is that you want me to get
it for you.

                    CROFT

You're the newbie. The new kid. The
rookie. Your one and only job as my
roommate is to do as I say. Play the
game right, and no one gets hurt.

                    SAMMY

I'm not going to get your coffee,
sorry. But while you're there, wherever
"there" is, would you mind getting me
a grape soda?

CROFT STARES AT SAMMY LIKE HE HAS TWO HEADS

                    CROFT
What did you just say?

                    SAMMY
Soda. Grape. Yummy.

SAMMY GOES BACK TO HIS UNPACKING, WHISTLING
WHILE HE WORKS. HE NOTICES CROFT STILL STARING
AT HIM.

                    SAMMY
Hey, let's just start over! (notices
Croft's angry look) Or not.

CROFT SUDDENLY SLAMS SAMMY'S SUITCASE SHUT.
SAMMY BARELY PULLS OUT HIS FINGERS IN TIME.

                    CROFT
Let's get one thing straight, Powell.
This is my world. You just live in it.

                    SAMMY
Your world. Check.

                    CROFT
Now get me that coffee.

SAMMY MULLS IT OVER, THEN FINALLY DECIDES HE'D
LIKE TO LIVE.

                    SAMMY
        I better make it two, in case you're
        extra thirsty.

AND SAMMY RUNS OUT TO BEGIN HIS NEW LIFE AS
CROFT'S SERVANT.

OASIS

WE WERE ABOUT FIFTEEN MINUTES
into the table read when I realized that maybe I could do
this after all.

It was the scene where Sammy meets his snob roommate, Croft Chandler. Croft tries to bully Sammy, but
Sammy fights back.

And when I read the line, "Soda. Grape. Yummy," the
strangest thing happened.

Dex laughed.

Adam Blankman smiled.

Becky Sue Woodcock patted me on the back.

Even Nano nodded. Slightly.

From that point on, I was able to relax, a little. And
about an hour and a half later, we were done. As I packed
up my script, people started coming over to shake my
hand.

"Nice job."

"Really funny."

"You got this."

I just kept saying "Thanks," over and over again.

Nano was the last to come over. "Solid start," he said, fiddling with his scarf. "Study your lines tonight, please. Tomorrow the real fun begins." Then he walked away, talking to some guy with headphones (like I said, everyone had headphones).

I looked at Ashley. "Tomorrow?"

"We start shooting," she said.

"Already?!"

"Yup. We rehearse as we go."

"Jeez." A pit formed in my stomach as I tried to imagine what that would be like. All those people with headphones and walkie-talkies staring at me! The most experience I'd had with a camera was when Eric Cunkler made an iPhone movie called *The Many Dumb Faces of Pete Milano*.

"You'll be fine," Ashley said.

"Or not," I said.

I heard a voice behind me. "Pete! Pete! Pete Milano!" I turned around and saw Shana walking quickly toward me, followed by some people who probably worked for her doing something, although I have no idea what that something was. The only guy I recognized was a giant guy named Hector, who was carrying Shana's tiny Chihuahua, named Bear. I think that was Hector's only job.

"Pete!" Shana sang out again.

Professional dog handler
(a full-time job)

So she finally remembered my name.

My first thought was that I'd done something wrong, that Shana decided there'd been a mistake and there was no way I could be in this movie with her. But before I could apologize for the terrible misunderstanding, she wrapped me in a big hug and kissed both my cheeks. (One at a time.)

"Pete! My goodness! You are very talented!"

"I am?"

"You sure are! Hey, can you come to my trailer for a few minutes? I want to show you something."

I looked at Ashley. She looked back at me like, *You don't say no to Shana Fox.*

"Uh, well I kind of need to get home to do homework, but sure, I guess for a little while."

"Great! Come with me."

"Pete's car will be here in ten minutes," Ashley said.

Shana rolled her eyes. "What is this, jail?" Then she giggled and tugged my arm. "Let's go."

We weaved through people, equipment, and tables of food as we worked our way to the other end of the studio lot. Finally, we turned the corner, and I saw what had to be one of the only pink mobile homes ever made. It was definitely the *biggest* pink mobile home ever made.

Picture this in pink

"Wow," I said. "It's . . . uh . . . it's really pink."

"I know," Shana said. "Isn't she gorgeous? My mom named her Oasis. I take her with me on every shoot."

"What does Oasis mean?"

"I'm not really sure," Shana said, scrunching up her face. "I think, like, vacation or something."

She gave her various assistants a quick glance, and they vanished like the wind. I followed her into the trailer and was nearly blinded by the amount of glitter covering everything—the couches, the mirrors, even the dog bowl.

"Take a seat," Shana said. I looked around before finally deciding to sit in a beanbag chair covered with pink fur.

"Thanks," I said. "Where's Hector taking Bear?"

"The manicurist."

"Oh."

We sat there for a minute, Shana just smiling at me.

"Was there something you wanted to talk to me about?" I asked.

She immediately burst into tears.

I couldn't believe it. "Shana! Are you okay? What happened?"

She answered with more sobbing.

"Was it something I said?" I asked, even though I hadn't said anything.

"My boyfriend hates me!" Shana wailed.

"Huh? What?"

"Dex! He totally hates me!"

I had the sudden feeling that I was somewhere I shouldn't have been, and I should probably leave immediately. But that feeling was quickly overwhelmed by *another* feeling, the one where I remembered I was sitting in a pink trailer with a blubbering Shana Fox, and this was going to make a great story to tell the guys back at school.

"I doubt that," I offered.

"He does! He totally ignored me during the table read. He thinks I'm too young for him, that I'm just a kid. I think he only liked me in the first place because I'm famous. Like, d'uh! Only the most famous person on the planet!"

Shana picked up a silk, golden-threaded handkerchief, which had the initials SAF sewn into it, and blew her nose loudly.

"Well, he's only sixteen and you're fifteen, right?"

"Actually, he's seventeen," she sniffled.

"Oh."

"Yeah," Shana said. She was starting to calm down. "It's better for actors' careers if we stay, like, young and innocent forever. And my parents and management team totally don't want me to date an older guy."

"Oh." I wanted to ask what a management team was, but was somehow able to stop myself.

Shana sniffled, then tried to smile. "How old are you?"

"Me?" I said, stalling. "Oh. Um, fourteen." Which was very close to true, since I was technically in my fourteenth year of life.

"Do you think I should break up with Dex?" Shana asked. By now she was sitting on the floor right next to my beanbag chair, twirling the little pink feathery things that hung down from the back.

"Uh . . . I don't really know, to tell you the truth."

Shana stood up suddenly. "Oh, Pete, you're so cute!" Then she bent over, kissed my cheek, and ran out of the trailer.

I waited a minute. Then another. And another.

Finally I stood up and went to the door. Ashley was standing there, reading her phone.

"I don't think she's coming back," I said.

Ashley nodded without looking up. "Ready for me to walk you to your car?"

"Yes, please."

And with that, my first day as a professional actor came to an end.

THINGS START TO GET WEIRD

WHEN I GOT HOME THAT NIGHT,
I wasn't Pete Milano, regular kid, anymore.

I was Pete Milano, movie star.

It started when I walked in the door. Two seconds later, my mom was running down the hall.

"Petey's home!" she shrieked.

"Mom? What are you doing here? Why aren't you downstairs at the restaurant?"

"I wanted to see my little boy!" she said, pinching my cheek.

I was confused. "Why are you acting like grandma?"

The next thing I knew, my *dad* was running down the hall.

"Petey!" His shriek was lower.

"Dad?! Huh? Seriously, what are you guys doing up here?" But he just shook his head, smiling and taking a video with his iPhone.

Sylvia was next, jumping into my arms like I was the

greatest brother in the world, as opposed to the brother who'd spent the last six years tickling her armpits until she couldn't breathe.

"Okay," I said, finally. "What's going on?"

The first family picture I've drawn where nobody's mad at me.

"We're just happy to see you, that's all!" said my mom.

But the real surprise was waiting in the kitchen, where Mareli was standing in front of a total feast.

"What's all this?" I asked. "What's going on?"

"I wanted to cook for you," she said. "I made all my favorite foods from back home. Plantains, mofongo, asopao. My mom helped me cook. I hope you like it."

"I love a woman who knows her way around a kitchen," said my mom. "Let's eat!"

We all sat down, and my dad pointed to his seat at the head of the table.

"I want you to sit there," he said. "It's a special occasion."

The food was a little weird, but I tried not to notice.

"Mmm, delicious," I said.

Then I noticed no one was talking. Everyone was just looking at me.

"So tell us what happened today!" Sylvia said.

"Was it fun?" asked my mom.

"How many famous people did you meet?" asked my dad.

More looking at me.

"It was good," I said. "But . . . uh . . . I actually . . ."

I stood up.

"I actually have a lot of lines to learn tonight, plus I have some homework, so I need to go study."

"Homework?" my dad said. I don't think he'd ever heard me use that word before. Which is because I never *had* used that word before.

"Yeah," I said. "Didn't mom tell you about our meeting

with Mrs. Sleep? I'm pretty sure she's going to be keeping an eye on me, so I need to make sure I keep up with my studies." Another word I'd never used.

"That makes sense," said Mareli, but she was clearly not thrilled.

Everything I was saying was true. I did have to learn my lines, and I did have homework, and Mrs. Sleep did say she wanted to be sure I could handle going to school half days.

But the real reason I wanted to go to my room?

I was uncomfortable.

Because here I was, the night before I was going to officially start acting in a big Hollywood movie—and for the first time in my life, I felt like I *didn't* want to be the center of attention.

What is *that* about?

ACTOR TO ACTOR

DID YOU KNOW that you can go through your whole middle school life and avoid some of the teachers entirely?

For example, there were two teachers—a science teacher, Mrs. Rensler, and a woodshop teacher, Mr. Cassano—whom I'd barely ever met. We would basically nod hello to each other in the hall, and that was about it.

But that was before I was Pete Milano, movie star.

"Hi there, Pete!" Mrs. Rensler said, as I shot baskets at recess. "Having a good day?"

"Sure, I guess," I said.

She beamed. "Terrific!"

Mr. Cassano didn't say hello. Instead, he held up his hand for a high-five as I walked down the hall between third and fourth periods.

"Dude!" he said.

Dude?

Never said one word to this guy

I slapped his hand. "Hey, Mr. Cassano."

"Great to see you!"

It had never been particularly great to see me before, but whatever.

"You too," I said politely.

But it wasn't until I was standing in the lunch line that I had my weirdest teacher moment of all. Mr. Twipple, the drama teacher, was gathering up the various nuts and berries he ate for lunch every day, when he looked up and saw me.

"Oh, hey Pete. Got a minute?"

"Uh, sure, I guess."

Mr. Twipple had never asked me for a second before, much less a minute. But that was then. This was now.

"Pete, have you ever thought about taking my drama class?"

Delicious food

The opposite of delicious food

I ate a French fry off my tray. "Not really."

"Well, I think it might be time," Mr. Twipple said. "Not only that, I want you to try out for the school play. It's called *The Race to Erase*, and it's about the man who invented the pencil eraser."

I tried not to laugh. Mr. Twipple was famous for his

shows. His last one—*Paper Tiger*, about the man who in-vented paper towels—featured dancing Kleenex.

"Well actually Mr. Twipple, I'm kind of busy these days."

"Of course you are!" He leaned in closer, and I noticed a kind of desperate look in his eyes. "Listen, Pete, I'm hav-ing a tough time getting the kids to go out for this one. Maybe it's the subject matter, I don't know. In my day, kids loved erasers—but now with all the computers and cell phones, they don't even know what an eraser is!" He took a sip of his carrot juice. "So anyway, think about it. Whatever you can do." He picked up his tray and scurried away.

Charlie Joe walked over from the chocolate milk sec-tion. "What was that about?"

"Mr. Twipple wants me to go out for his play."

"No way!"

"Way."

"Are you gonna do it? Coz if you will, I will."

I looked at Charlie Joe. Believe it or not, he had the same look in his eye that Mr. Twipple had. And Mrs. Rensler, and Mr. Cassano.

The look that says, *You're important, and I want you to like me!*

"Probably not," I told Charlie Joe. "Like I told Mr. Twip-ple, I'm really busy."

"Oh right," Charlie Joe said. "I get it."

And that was the moment I realized that things can change really fast. All of a sudden, I wasn't the obnoxious, annoying friend anymore. I wasn't the kid that people tolerated for entertainment value but didn't really consider a good friend. I wasn't the one asking the other kids what was going on after school. I wasn't on the outside looking in.

I was dead center. Smack in the middle!

It felt kind of awesome!

But—and it seems like there's always a *but*—the awesome part only lasted about half a day.

Which is when I went from being Pete Milano, movie star, to Pete Milano, the kid who thinks he's too cool to hang around with the regular people.

It started at the end of lunch, when Jake Katz and Nareem Ramdal asked me if I wanted to play video games after school, and I told them I couldn't, because I was shooting the movie.

It got worse between English and Math, when Timmy showed me a picture of his new trampoline and asked me if I wanted to come over the next day and try it out. I told him I couldn't, because I had a publicity photo shoot.

And then, during gym, Mareli reminded me we had plans to go to the mall on Saturday. Uh-oh. For that one, I just stalled.

It went on like that all day until science lab. Mr. Trenchler was going through the safety precautions for the 5,398th time when the hall monitor came in to pull me out of school.

Uh-oh.

As I made my way past all the other kids, I heard Charlie Joe say, "So let me get this straight: Pete's too busy to be our friend, but not too busy to skip science? Something's not right here."

I felt all the other kids looking at me the same way.

"Good luck with your first day of shooting," Mareli said. I smiled—at least I had one friend left.

"Thanks," I answered.

"You can tell me all about it at the mall on Saturday," she said.

I decided to come clean. "It turns out I can't go. I have to go to a costume fitting with Shana. It's the only day she can do it. I'm really sorry."

Mareli's face dropped. "Well, she's the star," she said, with an edge in her voice, "and we can't keep the star waiting. Thanks for telling me."

I couldn't get out of that classroom fast enough.

Like I said—things can change really quickly.

SAMMY AND THE PRINCESS, SCENE 13

INT. SCHOOL LIBRARY—DAY

SAMMY AND PRINCESS CLARISSA ARE STUDYING IN THE LIBRARY. SITTING ONE TABLE AWAY ARE CROFT CHANDLER AND HIS FRIENDS.

                    CLARISSA (Whispers)
          Those boys are being extremely noisy.

                    SAMMY
          They specialize in noise. They're pro-
          fessional noise specialists.

CLARISSA GIGGLES

                    CLARISSA
          You are funny. Thank you for making me
          laugh.

                    SAMMY
          Well, I'm a professional *laugh* special-
          ist. Happy to help.

CLARISSA LAUGHS AGAIN, A BIT LOUDER. THIS TIME, CROFT NOTICES. HE COMES OVER.

CROFT

Hey, what's so funny? Am I missing
something good over here?

SAMMY

Nah, we're just studying.

CROFT (Eyeing Clarissa)
I've noticed you around for a few
weeks, but I don't believe I've had the
pleasure of making your acquaintance.

CLARISSA

I'm sorry?

SAMMY

He's saying he wants to meet you.
(Sighs) Croft Chandler, I'd like you to
meet Clarissa . . . Clarissa . . . (He's
stumped by the length of her name)

CLARISSA STANDS UP

CLARISSA

Clarissa Du Roi. Nice to meet you.

CROFT AND CLARISSA SHAKE HANDS

                    CROFT

What kind of a name is Du Roi?

                    SAMMY

She's a pr—

            CLARISSA (Interrupting)
Proud transfer student!

*CROFT IS CHECKING CLARISSA OUT—AND HE LIKES
WHAT HE SEES*

                    CROFT

Well, hope you're enjoying Bainbridge
Prep, Clarissa. Tell me something,
though—why are you hanging around with
this kid? He's not exactly a superstar,
if you know what I mean.

                    CLARISSA

I like Sammy. He makes me laugh.

                    CROFT

Okay, well, whatever. (He winks at her)
We've got nothing but time, right? See
you around, Clarissa the proud transfer student.

*CROFT WALKS BACK TO HIS TABLE, STILL LOOKING
AT HER*

                    SAMMY (To Clarissa)
What was that about?

                         CLARISSA
What?

                         SAMMY
You didn't want to tell him you were a
princess?

                         CLARISSA
Of course not! I never want anyone to
know I'm a princess. Because people
treat you different. They want to be
around you for all the wrong reasons.
It's almost as if they don't care what
you're really like.

                         SAMMY
But I don't get it. You told me you
were a princess, like, five minutes
after I met you.

SHE LOOKS AT HIM INTENSELY

CLARISSA

I know. I guess I felt like I could
count on you or something. Like you
understood.

SAMMY LOOKS OVER AT CROFT, WHO IS POINTING AT
CLARISSA AND LAUGHING WITH HIS BUDDIES. SAMMY
SUDDENLY BECOMES DETERMINED TO PROTECT HER
FROM THEM.

SAMMY

You can definitely count on me. For
anything.

READY FOR NOTHING

THE FIRST THING I learned at the beginning of shooting was that they don't start at the beginning.

When I got to the studio, Ashley told me we were shooting the scene where Clarissa and Sammy bump into Croft at the library.

"But that's like, way into the movie," I said.

"Yup," Ashley answered. "Just another kooky thing about the movie business."

We headed over to the food table, which everyone called "craft services" for some reason. Dex was there, drinking some weird green drink.

"Yo, little man," he said to me. "Ready to rock and roll?"

"Yeah, I guess."

Dex pointed at a guy standing next to him. "Yo, this is Alex—he's playing Croft's buddy Darren."

Alex looked up midbite. "You must be Pete. Nice to meet you."

"Nice to meet you, too," I said, shaking Alex's hand. I

recognized him as the star of a TV series called *Abe Again*, about a boy who turns out to be the reincarnation of Abraham Lincoln. I thought it was pretty dumb, but the girls in school thought he was really cute.

"You look young," Alex said to me. "Like, actually young. Are you still in high school?"

The object of this drawing is older than he appears

"I wish," I said. "I'm still in middle school. What about you?"

Alex started cracking up. "I love this kid!" he shouted. "Nah, man. I wish I was in middle school, or in high school, or in any kind of school!" Then he leaned in, as if telling me a secret. "I'm twenty-three years old."

I stared at him. "Twenty-three? But . . . you're playing a kid."

"The miracle of anti-aging cream," Alex said. "That, and the fact that I come from a really short family."

"Wow," I said, still kind of shocked.

He shoved the last piece of bagel in his mouth. "Welcome to Hollywood, my young friend. Where everyone acts half their age—on screen and off."

I felt a hand on my shoulder. "You ready to shoot?" I looked up and saw Nano standing there, wearing a giant, red scarf.

"That's his shooting scarf, yo," Dex whispered.

"I'm ready," I said.

Nano adjusted his scarf. "Good." He sat down next to me. "Now, I need you to jump right into the deep end of the pool."

I was confused. "Wait, there's a pool?"

Nano sighed like he was talking to a three-year-old. "Not literally. I'm just saying, we're gonna need a good performance from you right away. That's how it works in the movies. I'm going to want a range of emotions from you in this scene. You're defiant but nervous—cocky but insecure. All good?"

I nodded, even though I had no idea what he was talking about.

"Okay. Come with me."

We walked toward the same building where we had the table read the day before. But when we walked inside, it looked like a completely different place. The giant empty room had been turned into a library. And when I say a library, I mean *an actual library*. There was no way you would think it wasn't real. There were tables, and chairs, and rows and rows of books. There was a giant desk in the middle with chairs for three librarians. And the amazing thing was, there were about fifty people in there *using the library*.

"Holy smokes," I said. "Who are all these people?"

Not a real library

"Extras," said Ashley.

"Extra what?"

"Extra people to fill out a scene," she explained. "You need them to make it seem realistic that it's an actual place."

I was amazed, but Nano didn't even notice. He was staring intensely at the row of computers.

"What kind of computers are these?" he barked.

Five people came scurrying over. They all looked scared. "Uh, I'm not quite sure," said one.

"I know what kind they are," Nano said, his voice rising. "The wrong kind."

They all answered with various versions of "So sorry" and "We'll replace them right away."

Nano watched them go, then turned back to me. "Okay, Pete. Ready to wow me?"

"I guess."

"Good. Go get dressed. See you in a couple of hours."

Huh?!

I stared at Ashley. "A couple of hours?"

Ashley chuckled. "You're getting off easy," she said.

HURRY UP AND . . . FAIL

THE SECOND THING I learned about shooting a movie was this: You wait.

Or, if you're like me, you doodle and make drawings while you wait.

You go to the wardrobe department and doodle while they pick out your clothes and fix them to fit you.

Then you go to the makeup department and doodle while they mess around with your hair, and you doodle some more while they put makeup on you, even though you're not a girl.

Then you go back to the wardrobe department and try the clothes on one last time to make sure they fit.

Then you go back to your dressing room, where you're told that someone will be coming for you really soon.

Then you wait. And doodle. And wait. And doodle.

Then, about two hours later, someone comes and brings you to the set.

My mother & sister would be
so jealous right now

Then it's time to shoot!

Or not.

Because you wait some more, while lighting guys tell you where to stand and the director gives you a bunch of directions that you don't understand, like, "Feel it, don't say it."

Then, FINALLY . . . it's time to shoot!

Or not.

No, wait.

It is.

It's for real this time.

* * *

"Okay, camera up!" Nano yelled.

I didn't know what that meant, but Shana, who had literally been asleep three seconds before, flashed me the brightest smile I'd ever seen.

"This is it, Paul," she whispered.

"Pete," I corrected her.

She giggled. "Right! My bad."

I closed my eyes and tried to remember everything Nano told me in rehearsal.

"ACTION!" Nano hollered.

"Those boys are being extremely noisy," Shana said, as Clarissa.

"They specialize in noise. They're professional noise specialists," I said, as Sammy.

"CUT!"

Nano came running over, scarf flapping. "No, for real this time, Pete. We're rolling."

"That was for real," I said.

Nano just looked at me. "Oh," he said.

"ACTION!"

"Those boys are being extremely noisy."

"They specialize in noise. They're professional noise specialists."

"CUT!"

I felt myself starting to sweat.

"Like we discussed," Nano said. "Cocky, but insecure."

"Right."

"ACTION!"

"Those boys are being extremely noisy."

"They specialize in noise. They're professional noise specialists."

This happened about twenty more times. I knew it was a problem when I saw the crew guys start to look at their watches.

Finally, after yet another "CUT!" Ashley intercepted Nano. "Mind if I talk to him for a second?"

"Be my guest," Nano muttered. "But hurry up. We have to get this shot or else we'll be over budget on the first day!"

Ashley pulled me aside.

"Ignore everything he said," she whispered.

My eyes bugged out. "Huh?"

"Just do it," Ashley went on. "I don't want to say anything bad about him, but the main reason he got this job is because his wife is Shana's dog walker, and Shana wouldn't do the movie without him. He doesn't know a thing about character."

"Okay," I said. "So . . . I should just say the lines?"

"Like you'd say them to your best pals back in the cafeteria in school," Ashley said. "Natural. Nice and relaxed. Simple as that."

"Let's go, people!" Nano said. Then he added, "The day's not getting any longer," whatever that meant.

Ashley started to scurry away, but I stopped her. "You're going to make a great director one day," I told her.

Ashley grinned. "Thanks."

"ACTION!" Nano barked.

The camera started whirring.

"Those boys are being extremely noisy," Shana said, for the umpteenth time.

But this time, when I looked at her, I didn't see Shana

Fox, superstar. I saw Timmy, and Charlie Joe, and Jake and Hannah and Katie.

"They specialize in noise. They're professional noise specialists," I said.

Shana (Clarissa) giggled.

I waited for Nano to yell, "CUT!"

But he didn't.

"Thank you for making me laugh," Shana (Clarissa) said.

"Well, I'm a professional laugh specialist," I said. Or should I say, Sammy said. "Happy to help."

And the cameras kept rolling.

And just like that, it was official.

I was an actor.

Act Three
ACTION!

IT'S LONELY AT THE TOP

SO, LIKE I WAS SAYING, it was official—I was
an actor.

As the days went by and the shoot went on, I settled
into a normal routine. Or, as normal a routine as you can
have when you're going to middle school and starring in a
movie at the same time. Basically, it went like this:

Go to school until one o'clock.

Get pulled out of class by the school monitor. Walk by
my friends, who are getting more and more jealous and
annoyed that I get to leave school early every day.

Walk outside, where a fancy Lincoln Town Car is waiting to take me to the movie studio.

Sit in the back seat and watch Ashley text the whole
time. I have nobody to text because everyone is still in
school, so I play games on my phone. They're fun but boring. (I know that might sound like it doesn't make sense,
but it does. Trust me.)

Get to the set, go into wardrobe, get dressed, get made

up, eventually get called to the set, actually *act* for approximately fifteen minutes, go back to the dressing room, wait some more, get called to the set again, shoot for another fifteen minutes.

Repeat that pattern five more times, until about seven o'clock.

Go home in Town Car. Ashley is still texting, but this time so am I. Answering texts, mostly.

I get a text from Mareli, who wants to study together for our social studies test (can't, have to memorize next day's lines).

I get a text from Charlie Joe, who wants to go to the mall and try every restaurant in the food court (can't, have to go take publicity pictures with Shana at some prep school upstate).

I get more texts from more people, who want to do more things, but my answer is always the same.

Can't.

Can't.

Can't.

One day, after a few weeks, Charlie Joe sends me a text: THIS IS CRAZY. YOU'RE NEVER FREE TO DO ANYTHING!

I text back: WELL, WHERE WERE YOU TWO MONTHS AGO, WHEN I WAS FREE EVERY DAY AFTER SCHOOL?

Charlie Joe: THAT'S TOTALLY NOT FAIR.

The gory details

Me: WHATEVER

Kids start to give up. Everybody wants to be my new best friend—but I don't have time to be *anybody's* best friend.

Eventually, Charlie Joe stops texting.

Timmy stops texting.

Even Mareli stops texting.

Go to school every day until one.

Get picked up early to go be in a movie.

It's so cool!

Until it isn't.

DELICIOUS FOOD, LOUSY CONVERSATION

"I INVITED MARELI over to dinner," my mom said, after I got home one night. We'd been shooting for around a month.

"You did?"

"Yup." Mom grabbed my backpack and got out my crumpled up lunch bag, which was unopened. The banana was completely flattened. "Ew," she said. "Why do I even bother?"

"I've told you a thousand times you don't need to make me lunch anymore," I said. "There's tons of food at the studio."

"But you don't get there until 1:45," said my mom. "Aren't you starving by then?"

"No offense, Mom, but I'd rather not ruin my appetite with tuna fish when I know I'm going to get steak an hour later."

"Fine," she said, dropping the broken banana into the garbage as if it were covered with mold.

"Why did you invite Mareli over?" I asked. "I'm kind of busy, in case you haven't noticed."

My mom looked at me. "What's going on with you? I remember when you found out she liked you—we couldn't wipe the smile off your face for weeks. Now suddenly you're too busy to have dinner with her?"

"It's complicated," I said, shrugging. I didn't really feel like going into the whole my-friends-are-all-mad-at-me-because-I'm-always-too-busy and I'm-mad-at-them-because-they-just-want-to-be-my-friend-because-I'm-in-a-movie thing. I knew my mom would ask me a ton of questions, and I was too tired to answer them.

"Everything's complicated," said my mom. "But, to answer your question, I saw Mareli downtown, and she looked at me with those big brown eyes and said how she hadn't really seen you around much lately, and then the next thing I knew, I was asking her over for dinner and she was saying yes." She hugged me. "Don't be mad. This is a good thing. You need to relax for just an hour or two and forget all the pressures of school and the movie and all that. You're still a kid, remember? So have dinner like a kid!"

"Okay. But I have to study my lines before dinner. Tomorrow we're shooting the scene where Sammy's roommate asks Princess Clarissa out."

"Oooh, sounds juicy," said my mom.

"See you at dinner," I said.

"Dinner's now," she said.

"What?"

"It's 7:30."

"No way."

I checked my phone—Mom was right.

Sheeesh. Two months ago, I literally had nothing to do. These days, I blinked, and it was dinnertime.

Times had sure changed.

The doorbell rang.

"Why don't you get it?" Mom asked me. But before I could, Sylvia came charging down the stairs and raced to the door.

"Mareli's here!" she squealed. Sylvia loved Mareli. I think they bonded over the same color nail polish.

When Sylvia opened the door, the first thing I noticed was that Mareli had completely changed her hair color. I'd never seen anyone in middle school do that before.

"Hi," I said.

"Hi," she said.

We stood there for a second, and then I said, "What happened?"

"Huh?" Mareli touched her hair self-consciously. "Oh, you mean this? I don't know, I just decided to try something different. So I went to the salon today, and the next thing I knew, I was a blonde."

She looked interesting, that's for sure, but there was something else. Something familiar. I tried to think where I'd seen that look before—dark skin and blond hair—and then it hit me.

Shana Fox.

"Are you trying to look like Shana?" I said, before I could stop myself.

Never question a girl about her hair

Mareli's face immediately turned bright red. "Of course not! What are you talking about?"

I tried to backtrack. "Nothing! I just meant, that you look really pretty, and you kind of reminded me of Shana, because of how pretty you are."

But Mareli wasn't buying it. "You think I'm trying to look like Shana? Why? Just because ever since you started being in that movie with her, you've been ignoring me? You think I'm jealous or something? Well, guess what? That's the craziest thing I've ever heard!"

As she was saying it, I realized something: That's *exactly* what I thought.

"No, of course that's not what I think," I said. "I just think it's funny that you and Shana have the same hair style, that's all."

"Coming here probably wasn't a great idea," said Mareli.

"Dinner's on the table!" called my mom.

We all sat down to eat, and I realized something else: We didn't have that much to talk about. We had a lot to NOT talk about, though. It seemed like every possible topic—the movie, Shana, school, friends—was some sort of minefield where something could explode at any minute.

So instead, we just talked about how delicious Mom's lasagna was, and Sylvia described every possible thing about the soccer game she'd played in that day.

"And I scored the winning goal!" she bragged, ending the description.

Mareli smiled. "That's fantastic!" she said. "You must have gotten your soccer skills from your brother."

Mareli was right—I was a pretty good soccer player. But I'd had to quit the team because of the movie—and of course, my teammates were mad at me about it.

Which is probably why Mareli mentioned it.

We sat there silent for another couple of minutes, until my mom brought up the one subject she knew would make everyone relax.

"Who wants dessert?" she said.

After we ate our peach cobbler, Mom asked Sylvia to

help her do the dishes. That left Mareli and me sitting there, by ourselves.

"Peter," Mareli began. Uh-oh. Whenever she called me "Peter," she meant business.

"Yeah?"

"I'm really happy for you that you are in this movie," she said. "You deserve it. I always knew you had something special in you."

I waited, because I knew there was a *but* coming.

"But," she went on, "when something this great happens, it can also mean some other things aren't so great. And we aren't so great. Because I feel like I'm getting in the way of your exciting new life."

"You're not," I said, trying to mean it.

"It's okay," Mareli said. "I know how busy you are, and how many interesting new people you're meeting. I can see how you have changed already—you're more responsible, more mature, much less of a troublemaker in school. It's great, seriously—and I'm sure it's crazy to think that in the middle of it all, you would still be thinking of your boring old life."

"You are not boring," I said. "You're the opposite of boring. And I'm not more mature. I don't *want* to be more mature! It's just that I'm really, really busy. And tired. But mostly busy."

The doorbell rang, which meant Mareli's mom was there to pick her up.

"Everybody's busy," Mareli said. "It's just that you're a different kind of busy." She got up. "I should go thank your mom for dinner. See you tomorrow."

As she walked into the kitchen, I wanted to tell her how wrong she was, but one thing stopped me.

She was right.

LEAVING A MARK

THE NEXT DAY WE PLAYED dodgeball in gym.

I know some schools don't allow dodgeball. They think it makes kids more violent or something. But luckily our gym teacher, Mr. Radonski, disagrees. He says the opposite is true: If you let kids burn off their aggressive energy playing sports, then they'll be less aggressive in life. That could be true. But I think the main reason Mr. Radonski lets us play is because he loves seeing kids peg balls at each other as hard as they can. Mr. Radonski is a little crazy.

"Okay, split up into two teams!" he barked. "Manning and Collins, you're captains."

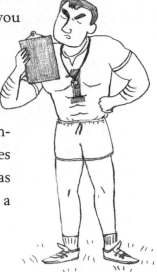

Just your average everyday lunatic gym teacher

Phil Manning was an obvious choice for captain, considering he was the strongest kid in the grade and wore a football jersey to school every day. Eliza Collins was a little less obvious, since the closest she came to playing sports was driving by soccer practice on the way to the hair salon. (Sure, I know some people consider cheerleading a sport, but as far as I'm concerned, if it doesn't involve a ball, it doesn't count.)

"Yay!" Eliza squealed. "I love being captain! Ladies pick first, right? I pick Pete."

"Me?" I said. I would have fallen off my chair, if I'd been sitting on one. In the old days, she was ready to have me arrested for stealing her pom-poms. But this wasn't the old days. This was the new days.

Charlie Joe chuckled. "Seriously? No offense, Eliza, but Pete's worse than me at dodgeball. And I'm pretty bad."

"He may even be worse than *me*," Jake added. "And dodgeball is like my forty-third best sport."

"What does that even mean?" Timmy said, scratching his head.

"It means I stink at dodgeball," Jake said.

I took my place behind Eliza and tried to ignore the chatter.

"I pick Jeff," Phil announced. Jeff Santore was known for having the best arm in the grade. When he nailed you, it left a mark.

Eliza and Phil kept picking until the teams were set. Then Mr. Radonski blew his whistle, and the fun began.

"Gotcha!"

"Ow!"

"You're out!"

"That missed!"

"You're dead meat!"

"My sister throws harder than that!"

And so on.

Finally, we were down to four people. By some miracle, I was one of them. My teammate Eric Cunkler was still in, too. On the other side, Charlie Joe and Jeff Santore were left.

"Five minutes to the bell!" Mr. Radonski hollered. "Let's get this thing done!"

Eric and I were hugging the back wall, basically hiding, while Jeff and Charlie Joe were busy making a plan.

Mr. Radonski saw us and blew his whistle. "Hey! Milano and Cunkler, no cowering! Get out there and play the game like men!"

Oh, sure, that was easy for Mr. Radonski to say. He was on the sidelines, far away from Jeff Santore's deadly right arm.

Eric was clearly thinking the same thing. "Too bad we can't peg Mr. Radonski," he said.

Which gave me an idea.

It was a pretty crazy idea, but I was known for my crazy ideas. At least, I used to be. At first, I told myself to forget it. But then I thought about Mareli saying I'd changed . . . That I matured . . .

Well, I've got news for you.

No one says I've matured until *I* say I've matured.

"Mr. Radonski!" I whispered. "Come quick. I think there's blood on the floor!"

That scared Mr. R. The last thing he needed was for a kid to get hurt on his watch. As he hurried out to the floor to take a look, I threw the ball as hard as I could toward Jeff, who was still huddled up with Charlie Joe, but I missed—on purpose. The ball whacked against the back wall. Then, as Jeff whirled around and got ready to fire back, I ducked behind Mr. Radonski. Not only would Jeff miss me, he'd nail Mr. R. Now that's what I call a win-win.

I was already congratulating myself. It had seemed like a great plan thirty seconds earlier, when I'd thought of it.

The only problem was, even though Mr. Radonski didn't see any blood on the floor (because there wasn't any), he did spot what appeared to be a three-year-old piece of chewed gum.

"That's disgusting!" he thundered. "Who did this to my gym?"

Then he kneeled down to try and scrape it off . . . which left me standing there.

Just in time for Jeff to fire.

As that bright red rubber ball screamed through the air, I did what anyone who sees something coming right for them would do.

I screamed.

THWACK!

I think the whole school heard the sound of that ball hitting the right side of my face.

"OOOOOWWWWW."

I crumpled to the floor. A few girls screamed. Everybody ran over.

"Stand back!" Mr. Radonski bellowed. "Give him some room!" He bent down. "You okay, kid? You took quite a shot there." Then he set his sights on Jeff Santore. "You nailed him right in the face! What's the matter with you?"

"I'm really sorry," Jeff said, petrified. "He fired and I just fired back. I didn't mean it."

"Go tell Mrs. Sleep you didn't mean it," Mr. Radonski ordered.

Poor Jeff.

But also, poor me. I sat there, rubbing the side of my face. I was just glad it was still there.

"Are you okay?" Eliza said, bending down.

"I said give him room!" yelled Mr. Radonski.

"I'm his captain!" Eliza fired back. That one stumped Mr. Radonski, so he let her stay.

"Can I ask you something?" Eliza said to me.

I continued rubbing. "Sure."

"Are you shooting your movie today?"

That seemed like a weird, irrelevant question. "Uh, yeah. Why?"

She took out a little mirror and handed it to me. (Why she had a mirror in her gym shorts, I'll never know.)

I looked into it and saw that my cheek and eye had swollen up to approximately the size of Colorado.

"I think you're gonna need a little extra makeup," Eliza said.

SHELDEN FELDON DOESN'T SMOKE A CIGAR

BY THE TIME I got to the studio that day, the swelling had gone down a lot. But still Ashley took one look at me and started texting like a madwoman.

Five minutes later, Sheldon Felden walked in.

"Jeez, that was fast," I said.

"Hey, kid," Mr. Felden said. "How do you like being a movie star so far?"

"The movie's not even out yet, sir."

"I'm hearing good things."

He walked over to me and examined the bruise on my face. Then he took out a cigar and started rolling it around his fingers. "I know it's a lot of pressure, trying to be in school and be in a movie and keep a level head. You managing okay?"

"I'm doing good," I told Mr. Felden.

"'Well,'" he corrected. "Doing *well*."

"Right. Doing well, sir."

"Terrific." He sat down with a big, old-man sigh. "But

here's the thing, kid. You got responsibilities now. Big ones. And you can't be out there acting like a dumb kid. You hear what I'm saying?"

"Yes, sir."

"So what happened? You get in a fight with your girlfriend?"

"No, sir. Dodgeball accident."

Mr. Felden laughed and coughed at the same time. "Dodgeball! Good stuff. Well, after makeup takes care of it, we should be okay. Just don't let it happen again."

"Yes, sir."

"Stop calling me sir, like I'm a drill sergeant, for crying out loud!" he barked, kind of like a drill sergeant. He pushed himself out of his chair and headed to the door. "Have a good day. Give me a holler if there's anything I can do to help you out. And don't let Nano scare you. He's a nitwit." He winked. "Just don't tell anyone I said that, or I'll get fired."

That was pretty funny, since we both knew that the only person who could fire anyone around there was Sheldon Felden himself.

SHANA

I WALKED TO THE SET, a fake chemistry class-room, where we were going to shoot the scene where Sammy messes up his science project and Clarissa helps him fix it. Shana was already there, waiting for the lighting to be tweaked. (*Tweak* is pretty much the most popular word on a movie set, BTW. "Need to tweak the script." "Need to tweak the costume." "I like your tweaks." "We just need to give it one more tweak.")

She was on the phone, as usual.

"Dex?" I whispered.

She nodded, without looking at me. Shana's relationship with Dex seemed pretty complicated: One day they were texting and talking and flirting and giggling, the next they wouldn't even look at each other, unless they were shooting a scene together.

As Louie the stagehand put it, "You get used to it."

Finally, Shana glanced up and noticed my face,

which—even with makeup—still had a very visible bruise on it.

"Whoa, what happened to you?"

I shrugged.

Shana took a closer look. "Dang, the lighting guys are going to have to work overtime today. Fight with your girlfriend?"

"Nah, dodgeball," I said.

"Too bad," Shana said. "Fight with your girlfriend is a better story for the press."

Shana was obsessed with the movie websites and magazines. She had kind of a love/hate relationship with all the reporters and photographers that followed her around. I guess all celebrities do.

"Well," I said, "maybe the press will be fascinated to know that Mareli had dinner at my house last night, and it didn't go that well."

This got Shana's attention. She was a big gossip just like everybody else. "How come?"

I sighed. "I don't really know. She thinks I'm too full of myself because I'm in a movie, and that I don't want to hang out with her anymore. And all my friends agree with her."

"Well, tough," Shana said. "They're just going to have to get used to it."

I hesitated a second, then said, "And I think she's a little jealous of you." That made Shana giggle, so I quickly added, "Which is totally ridiculous, d'uh. As if you would ever like someone like me."

"Well you never know," Shana said, giving me that flirty smile I recognized from the poster that's on thousands of bedroom walls—including my little sister's. "Dex doesn't have that cute dimple on his left cheek like you do."

"Great," I said. "Cute left dimple. Good to know."

Shana laughed. "See? Clarissa the Princess is right—you are funny!"

"And Sammy is right, too," I said. "You are pretty. Really pretty."

"What's going on over here?" a voice behind us said. I turned around, and Dex was standing there, looking down at me like I was one of those weird granola bar things he liked to eat.

"Uh, nothing," I said. "Shana and I were just talking about my girlfriend."

"That's right," Shana said. Then she winked at me. Which Dex saw.

"Your girlfriend?" He said. "*Your* girlfriend? Sure you weren't talking about *my* girlfriend?"

"I thought I wasn't your girlfriend anymore," Shana said.

"Depends on the day," Dex told her, giving her a kiss on

the cheek. Then, looking at me, he added, "And you keep your girl troubles to yourself."

Shana watched him walk away with a look of half love and half hate. Then she turned to me and said, "I have an idea. I want you to come to dinner with me."

"Huh?"

"My family is coming into town next week to celebrate the end of shooting, and I want them to meet you. How about Friday night?"

I stared at Shana. Sure, we were getting along pretty well. And yeah, maybe we had a flirty moment there for a second. But she had a boyfriend! Kind of. And I had a girlfriend! Kind of.

Not to mention the fact that she was Shana Fox.

"You mean, like a date?"

"Call it what you want," Shana said, batting her eyelashes.

I gulped. "Um, okay. Where?"

"Doesn't your family own a restaurant?"

The thought of Shana eating at Milano's Pizza and Pasta both thrilled and terrified me.

"Well, yeah . . . but it's like totally not fancy. In fact, it's the opposite of fancy."

"Perfect!" Shana flashed a smile. "I love the opposite of fancy!"

"Great." I made a mental note to tell my parents that

Milano's had to look like a five-star restaurant next Friday night.

As we got final touch-ups from the makeup department, she held up her phone. "Look at this selfie Dex just sent me!" she said. "So adorable!"

If anyone ever tells you girls are easy to figure out, they're lying.

THE RETURN OF IRIS

I WALKED BACK to the dressing room, thinking about the fact that I had just accepted an invitation to have dinner at my parents' restaurant with one of the most famous girls in America. I stopped to graze at the craft services table, with my eye on the mini Snickers bars. They were the crew's favorite, but none of the other actors ate them. Apparently actors and chocolate don't mix. Which is a total waste, since movie sets have some of the greatest chocolate treats known to man.

I grabbed a handful and started walking to my dressing room. Suddenly I heard a familiar voice behind me.

"Pete! Wait up!"

I turned to see a woman running toward me, balancing two purses, with a third bag over her shoulder. It took me a second to figure out who it was, until the two cell phones gave it away.

"Iris!" I said happily.

It had only been a few months since I first met Iris Galt

at Just Brew It, where she asked me, totally out of nowhere, if I wanted to try out for a movie. But it may as
well have been a lifetime.

"Pete Milano! How are
you? It's a long way from
the coffee shop up in Eastport, isn't it?"

We hugged. "Yup, I'm back," she went on. "The woman
you have to thank for all this!" She winked. "Or blame,
depending on how it's going."

"It's going good," I said. "I mean, it's going well."

She smiled at me like she was my best friend and
my aunt, all at the same time. "I hope so, Pete. I know the

schedule is brutal, and it's not exactly all fun and games. But in the long run, this will be an opportunity of a lifetime."

"I know."

"I'll bet you miss your friends, huh?" Iris asked. "This life is a little crazy."

"Yeah, kind of."

"And the people are a little crazy."

"Yeah, definitely."

"You'll get used to it," she said. "Every kid who goes into the movie business thinks they'll never be able to find a way to leave their old life behind. And yeah, it's hard at first. But that's okay. Because you know something? This new life is way more exciting! You'll discover that soon enough, just like every kid actor who came before you."

"Leave my old life behind?" I asked.

"Well, pretty much," Iris said. "That's what happens when you become a movie actor."

I thought about that.

Hold on a second.

Yeah, my friends could be a pain in the neck. And yeah, things with Mareli were a little hairy at the moment. But *leave them behind*? Forever?

That would stink.

"Iris, can I ask you something?"

"Sure."

"Mr. Felden asked me this morning if there was

anything he could do to make things a little easier for me. I'm sure he was just being polite, but actually, I thought of something."

Iris looked at me and waited.

"I notice they use a lot of extras in this movie," I said. "And a lot of extras who are kids." I stopped and took a breath. "Maybe some of my friends could help out."

"Help out?" Iris asked.

"You know," I said. "Like be extras? In the movie?" I saw the surprised expression on her face and added, "Only if they need more people, of course."

Iris stopped walking. And since she had my arm linked with her arm, I stopped walking. She looked like she was thinking.

"Well, we are moving to our location shots for the last week of the shoot," she said. "We're going to be up in Eastport. And I've been hearing about how you bring authenticity to your scenes. Adding a few of your friends might make it feel even more real." Iris took out one of her two phones and started typing. "I'll find you later, and you can give me some names. I'll want to get press in on this, they might like the local angle." Her other phone buzzed. "Oh good, it's Sheldon," she told me. "I'll talk to him about it. He may actually go for this."

"Really?" I couldn't believe what I was hearing. All I could think was, *Wait until I tell the guys!*

Iris hopped in a golf cart that I didn't even realize was

next to us. "If we're going to use your pals, it will be for the scene at Jookie's," she said. "I'm looking forward to visiting your town again! Especially that coffee shop. Their espresso is delish!" Then she drove away.

"Holy moly," I said to myself. As I walked up to my dressing room, I saw the door fly open. Ashley popped out and ran over to me.

"Pete, where have you been?"

"I was talking to Iris," I told her.

"About what?"

"I asked her if some of my friends could be in the movie."

"Are you serious?"

I grinned. "Yup. She's checking with Sheldon to see if it's cool."

But instead of grinning, too, Ashley shook her head. "I'm not sure about this," she said. "I'm not sure about this at all."

"Why not?"

Ashley sighed. "Iris is convinced that Nano only got the directing job because he's married to Shana's dog walker, and Nano is convinced that Iris only got her producing job because Sheldon Felden was college roommates with her uncle. So of course, they hate each other. This will probably start a huge fight."

"Oh," I said. "Well, she told me she'd get back to me later. Do you want me to tell her never mind?"

"No," Ashley said, shaking her head. "If Iris has already talked to Sheldon, it's too late. And if Sheldon thinks it's a good idea, then it's officially a good idea."

She walked away, muttering. I couldn't quite tell what she was saying, but it sounded something like, "I knew I should have gone to dental school."

MATH PROBLEM

THAT NIGHT, Ashley texted to tell me the plan was a go.

The next day at school, I couldn't wait to tell everyone. I counted the seconds until lunch. This was going to be good. I was going to be a total hero.

"I have an announcement to make," I announced, five seconds after everyone sat down.

Everyone at the table looked up.

"You'll no longer be signing autographs?" asked Charlie Joe.

"Ha-ha," I said.

"You're changing your name to Marlon Brando Milano?" Katie suggested. I didn't know what that meant.

"Knock it off, you guys, I'm serious." I waited for a second, to let the drama build (Shana taught me that). Then I looked at Mareli, to make sure she was paying attention. She was.

"Okay, here goes: Who wants to be in the movie?"

Everyone stopped eating, mid–fish stick.

"What do you mean, be in the movie?" asked Charlie Joe. He was always the fastest to recover from a shocking piece of news.

"I mean, I asked the producers if you guys could be in the movie, and they said yes."

"I don't believe you," said Timmy.

"Neither do I," agreed Jake Katz. "That seems weird, that a movie producer would agree to let some actor's friends be in his movie."

"Sheldon Felden would," I insisted. "And Sheldon Felden did. So who wants to?"

Nobody moved.

"I'm *serious*!"

"I think it's safe to say that all of us would want to be in your movie," Katie Friedman said.

"Great!" I said. I waited for everyone to thank me and tell me how awesome I was.

I kept waiting.

"What are we going to do in the movie?" Jake asked finally.

"Oh, right," I said. "Well, we're shooting a scene at Jookie's, and you'll be in the scene as, like, regular people who hang out at Jookie's, you know, just doing normal stuff while the scene is happening."

"You mean, like extras?" said Nareem Ramdal.

I was shocked. "Yes! You know what extras are?"

Nareem looked insulted. "Of course I know what extras are. I am a big fan of the Bollywood movie tradition, in which extras play a vital if underappreciated role."

"So what do they do?" asked Charlie Joe.

"Nothing," answered Nareem, before I could think of a better way to put it.

"So let me get this straight," Mareli said, speaking for the first time. "You want us to be in the movie, barely noticeable and doing nothing, while you get to sit there and flirt with Shana Fox?"

"Well, not doing nothing, technically," I corrected her, which didn't seem to help. I felt my face turn red. "Why does everything have to come back to Shana? I can't help it if she's in the movie with me!"

"Maybe not," said Mareli. "But you don't have to rub my face in it all the time."

"I'm not! I swear!"

Mareli stared at me. "Okay, let's just forget it," she said. Then she tried to smile, and walked away.

I tried to smile, too. "I just thought it would be fun," I said to the rest of the guys.

Katie came up to me. "That's actually really nice," she said. "We appreciate it. We really do."

"And it does sound fun," said Timmy. "A real movie! Cool. Thanks, Pete."

The more the guys talked about being in the movie, the more excited they got about it. But the one person who I actually wanted to make happy, was somewhere else—being not happy.

Maybe Iris was right.

Maybe I *was* leaving my old life behind and didn't even know it.

SAMMY AND THE PRINCESS, SCENE 22

INT. *SCHOOL DINING HALL—DAY*

SAMMY AND CLARISSA ARE EATING TOGETHER. CROFT CHANDLER APPROACHES THEIR TABLE

>   CROFT
> Hey, guys, what's going on?

>   CLARISSA
> Hello.

>   SAMMY (Uneasy)
> Hey.

CROFT ZEROES IN ON CLARISSA

>   CROFT
> So, hey, yeah, the year is almost over
> and I still feel like I don't know you.
> Like, just because maybe I was a
> little rude the first time we met, you
> still hold it against me.

>   CLARISSA
> I do not.

CROFT

Well, either way, I'm sorry about that.

CLARISSA (Surprised)

Yes. Well, that is very nice of you to
say. I appreciate it, thank you.

SAMMY

Nice chatting with you, Croft.

*THEY WAIT FOR CROFT TO WALK AWAY, BUT HE
DOESN'T.*

CROFT

So, anyway, Clarissa, the Spring Dance
is coming up, and I was wondering if
maybe you wanted to go with me.

CLARISSA

Wow. That is so very kind of you, but
I can't.

CROFT

Why not?

CLARISSA

I will be with Sammy at his home.

                    CROFT
Seriously? You guys aren't going to the
Spring Dance?

                   CLARISSA
I have always wanted to spend a day
with a nice American family in a nice
American town, and since we have no
school that day, it seemed like a good
opportunity.

                    SAMMY
That's okay. You can go with Croft if
you want.

              CLARISSA (Sharply)
Sammy! (To Croft) I am sorry, but I
cannot.

CROFT SHAKES HIS HEAD, IN SHOCK THAT SOMEONE
WOULD ACTUALLY TURN HIM DOWN

               CROFT (To Sammy)
What's your friend's deal? Why doesn't
she ever tell anyone where she's from?
Or how she ended up here?

SAMMY IS TONGUE-TIED.

> CLARISSA (Jumping in)
> My father was transferred here for work.

> CROFT (Suspicious)
> Really? What's his job?

> CLARISSA (Trying to change
> the subject)
> Perhaps we can go to an event another time?

> CROFT
> Yeah, whatever. See you around.

CROFT LEAVES. SAMMY IS EMBARRASSED BUT TRIES TO LAUGH IT OFF

> SAMMY
> "Perhaps we can go to an event another time?" Seriously? That was appalling! I'm appalled!

CLARISSA

Sammy. You must not be so scared of
him. He is an obnoxious fool.

SAMMY

A rich, obnoxious fool who's twice my
size.

CLARISSA

He will never hurt you, I promise.

SAMMY

Wait a second—I'm the one that's supposed to be saying that to you!

CLARISSA

We are supposed to say it to each
other.

CONFUSION

FINALLY IT WAS FRIDAY—the last day of shooting in the studio, before we moved to the locations in Eastport.

We were doing the scene where Croft asks Clarissa out in the dining hall. Shana and Dex weren't speaking to each other off camera—she was still mad at him for dissing her a few days earlier—and so it was a little bizarre watching them fight on camera. And what was even stranger was that as my character got upset and jealous, it started to feel like it was *me* getting upset and jealous.

According to Ashley, that's called "art imitating life."

As soon as we wrapped for the day, Dex just left without saying goodbye. Shana tried to pretend everything was normal, but you could see the anger in her eyes. She shook her head, then smiled at me and said, "Are you as excited for dinner tonight as I am?"

As if things weren't crazy enough.

"Oh yeah, definitely." I started taking off the jacket and

tie I had to wear for almost every scene (remind me never to go to private school, by the way). "Uh, so tell me again why we're having this dinner?"

"My family's in town, remember?" Shana chirped. "They'll think you're cute."

"What about Dex? Is he coming?"

She rolled her eyes. "Yeah, no."

She was acting like she couldn't care less about him. But for some reason, I didn't quite believe her.

Maybe she wasn't as good of an actress as I thought.

THE SOUND CAKE MAKES WHEN IT HITS HUMAN SKIN

"WOW!" SAID MY SISTER SYLVIA. "This place looks amazing!"

She was talking about my parents' restaurant. And she was right—it was practically unrecognizable. Everything looked shiny and new—the plates, the glasses, the silverware, even the cheese shakers.

Get this—my dad actually put *tablecloths* on the tables.

"Totally amazing!" my sister said again, louder. She was practically vibrating with excitement, because she was finally going to get to meet Shana Fox.

"You can't act like an idiot in front of her," I said to Sylvia.

My mom gave me a look. "Don't talk to your sister that way."

"Yeah," Sylvia said, smacking me.

"Ow!" I howled. "You can't hit me like that! I'm a movie star now!"

My mom rolled her eyes. "Oh, for crying out loud."

Actual tablecloths

"Well, I am," I said. "Sheldon Felden told me so himself."

"I'm going to give you a pass because of the big dinner tonight," my mom said. "You're probably a little nervous."

"Nervous? That's crazy," I said, laughing nervously.

"Well, we've got everything ready to go," said my mom. "The restaurant is already crowded. We've got the full staff working tonight."

I eyed Sylvia. "Did you tell anyone that Shana was eating at the restaurant tonight? Or post something online?"

"Of course not!" she said. Then she whacked me in the arm again. "That's for not trusting me."

"You are so gonna get it after dinner," I told her.

My mom was right: The place was packed. Like, not just crowded. I mean, it was mobbed. Every table was filled, and there was a huge line that went out the door. There were people everywhere.

There's no way our pizza is THAT good

"This is weird," I said to myself. Somebody had obviously spilled the beans about Shana coming. But the only people I had told were my family.

"Where are we supposed to sit?" I asked my mom.

"Over there." She pointed at a huge, empty table in the middle of the restaurant. A big sign on it said, "Reserved."

"Isn't that a little obvious?" I said.

"I have a feeling Shana wants to be seen," my mom said. "Her people came in, and they decided where to sit." She kissed us both. "I'm going to see how your father is doing in the kitchen. I'll be back in a bit."

Sylvia and I sat down at the table. I checked my phone—7:25. Shana and her family were supposed to get there in five minutes.

Twenty minutes later, they still weren't there, and I was getting really tired of everyone staring at us.

"Are you sure they're coming?" Sylvia whined, for the sixty-second time.

"Stop asking me that."

Fifteen minutes later, I found my parents, who were talking to someone at the bar. "Are you sure they're coming?" I asked them.

My parents looked at each other. "How are we supposed to know?"

Finally, an hour late, the door to the restaurant swung open and two huge guys walked in. I recognized one of them as Shana's bodyguard from the set. The other guy

I'd never seen before. They went up to my parents and started talking to them. My dad pointed to our table.

"I think she's here," I whispered to Sylvia.

Sure enough, thirty seconds later the door opened again, and there she was. Shana Fox, the world's biggest girl superstar, came walking into Milano's Pizza and Pasta just like a regular person! Even though I knew it was going to happen, I still couldn't believe it. Right behind her were two people that must have been her parents, because they were older and looked a little worn out. It occurred to me that worrying about your daughter being gawked at, written about, and pawed over must be a pretty exhausting way to live.

Everyone in the restaurant kind of stopped talking at the same time. People pretended not to stare at her, but that just made it more obvious that they were.

I waved. Shana saw me and waved back.

"Oh my God Oh my God Oh my God," Sylvia said.

By the time Shana and her parents got to the table, my parents had somehow materialized right next to me.

"Hi, I'm Anna Milano, and this is my husband, Vince," said my mom. "It's our pleasure to welcome you to Milano's."

"I'm Jim Fuchs," said Shana's dad. "Thanks for having us."

"I'm Erica," said her mom.

"I'm Pete," I said to them.

Shana grinned. "And I'm Shana!"

"D'uh," said Sylvia, and everyone laughed. Sylvia stared at Shana and said, "Why do you have a different last name from your parents?"

Shana shrugged. "Can't remember. Some agent or manager decided a long time ago that Fox sounds better. It still says Fuchs on my birth certificate, though."

"Cool!" Sylvia said.

We all sat down, trying to pretend that everyone else in the restaurant wasn't watching our every move.

"I'm sorry it's so crazy in here," said my mom.

Shana's dad shrugged. "Part of the deal," he said. "We're used to it."

"Pete, have you been having a good time being in the movie?" asked Shana's mom.

"Absolutely," I said. "It was really scary at first but now it's great. Shana has been really helpful."

"You don't have to say that," Shana said.

I nodded. "But it's true."

Sylvia was still staring at Shana. "My brother talks about you all the time," she said. "Shana this, Shana that. I think he might have a crush on you."

"Sylvia!" I said.

"He even drew a picture of you to give you as a present," she added.

Shana grinned. "You did?" she asked.

I froze. The truth was, I *had* drawn a picture—but all of a sudden I felt shy about it.

"Give it to her," Sylvia said.

I smacked her on the arm. "Quiet!"

"Petey!" said my dad.

"Ow!" Sylvia moaned. "That really hurt." Then she tried to hit me back, but her arm knocked over the root beer, which spilled all over Mrs. Fuchs.

"Oh, my goodness!" yelled my mom.

Sylvia burst into tears. "It's all Pete's fault!"

The moment things
start to go south

"This is going well," Shana said, giggling, as everyone tried to clean up the mess. Other people in the restaurant were staring. I noticed Charlie Joe's sister, Megan, and her boyfriend, two tables over. They laughed and waved.

"Well, Sylvia, it's funny you should bring up your brother having a crush on me," Shana said. "Because this seems as good a time as any to announce that Pete and I are boyfriend and girlfriend."

Huh?

Sylvia screamed.

My parents looked shocked.

Shana's parents looked like nothing could shock them anymore.

"Wait, what?" I said.

"We're boyfriend and girlfriend," Shana repeated. "Isn't it great?"

"We are?"

Shana took my hand. "I thought we should tell people now, sweetie, since we're almost done shooting the movie."

Sweetie?! The only one who ever called me "sweetie" was my Great Aunt Rose.

"I don't remember us saying we were boyfriend and girlfriend," I protested, weakly.

Shana batted her eyelashes at me. "You mean you don't wanna be?"

I could feel the whole restaurant looking at us. I thought about what my life used to be like, when I couldn't even get any of my so-called friends to come with me to the mall, and now here I was—a star in a movie, with one of the most famous girls on the planet asking me to be her boyfriend.

And then I thought about Mareli, and how she told me maybe it was best for the both of us if we just moved on.

"No, I mean yeah, I do, I guess," I said. "I do wanna be boyfriend and girlfriend."

"Great!" Shana exclaimed.

Then she signaled to the big bodyguard guy I'd never seen before, and he opened the front door to the restaurant, and about twenty people with cameras rushed in.

The cameras started going wild. In fact, there were so many clicks, and flashes, and people, that it took a minute for me to notice Mareli coming through the door, holding something in her hands.

Behind her was the whole gang: Hannah, Katie, Charlie Joe, Eliza, Timmy, Nareem, and Jake.

Mareli smiled at me. I smiled back. They all waved. I waved back. They started walking toward me.

"Mareli's here," I said to Shana. "We need to hold off on this whole—"

Which is when Shana kissed me.

Right on the lips.

Uh-oh.

CLICK! CLICK! CLICK! FLASH! FLASH! FLASH!

Mareli's smile vanished as she walked faster.

"This isn't what it looks like," I shouted to her, in case she could hear me through the noise.

Kiss of death

It wasn't until she was right next to me that I could tell what she was holding. It was a cake.

"Wow, is that for me?" I said. "I thought you were, like, totally mad at me."

"I was," she said. "And I baked you a cake because I wanted to say I'm sorry."

My eyesight was still recovering from all the camera flashes, which must have caused weird sparks to go off in my brain. How else can I explain the amazingly stupid thing I said next?

"I accept your apology," I told Mareli.

Under normal circumstances
I'm a big fan of chocolate coconut cake

THWOP!

That's the sound that cake makes when it hits human skin, by the way. I know that for a fact, because Mareli's answer to my incredibly dumb comment was to pick up a big hunk of cake and throw it in my face.

"Wha?" I said, through the icing.

But Mareli didn't say a word. I guess she figured she would let her arm do the talking, because three seconds later, she did it again.

THWOP!

"By the way," she hissed, "you never even kissed me *once*." Then she turned around and walked away.

I think I was in shock, because everything after that was a blur. Here's what I remember: My parents trying to get the photographers to leave, but failing; Shana's parents both on their phones, probably calling her "management team"; Sylvia texting every friend she had; and me realizing that the cake was chocolate, with coconut frosting, and it was pretty darn tasty.

I snapped out of it when Shana elbowed me in the ribs.

"Wanna get out of here?" Shana asked.

"More than anything ever," I answered.

"Is there a back way?"

"Unfortunately not."

Shana laughed, like she couldn't believe what a dumpy little restaurant she'd found herself in. Then, without another word, she put her hand over her eyes and headed out, crouching low behind her security guys. I realized I wanted to hide, too—or, at least, somehow avoid making eye contact with everyone I'd disappointed.

So I pulled out my sunglasses—you know, the ones that my friends gave me to congratulate me for getting cast in the movie—and put them on. Then I walked past those very same friends, my family, the photographers, and all the rest of the people who'd come to gawk at a famous person and got way more than they bargained for.

* * *

As soon as we made it out, Shana dragged me into the alley next to the restaurant, where her limo was waiting.

"Wow!" she said. "That was kind of awesome!"

"Kind of awesome?" I said. Then a little louder: "KIND OF AWESOME?! That was not awesome! That was horrible!" I heard her get a text, and she quickly checked her phone. "Are you even listening?" I yelled. "Practically everyone I know is inside there! Including the girl I've liked for like, forever! And now everything is ruined!"

"Oh, Pete," Shana said, "I'm so sorry." But she didn't exactly *look* sorry.

"I'm not sure it's such a good idea for us to go out," I told her. "I hope you don't mind."

Shana giggled a little bit before she was able to stop herself. "Listen, I feel bad you're sad. I don't want you to be sad. But, I guess I should explain: You and me aren't really going out. It's just a scheme I cooked up with my press team, to get some more publicity for the movie. Plus, I knew it would make Dex super jealous. And it worked! It's already up online, and that was him, texting me! We're back together!"

Then she started typing. "Hey," she said to herself as she typed, "it got a little crazy but everything worked out. All good. X-X-X." She paused. "O-O-O." She pushed one last button. "And . . . send."

Then she gave me a hugless hug—you know, the kind that feels empty inside—and got in the back of her limo.

"See you tomorrow, boyfriend!" she yelled as she drove away.

I watched her go. Then I took my sunglasses off, walked upstairs to my room, and went to bed.

Act Four

EVERY MOVIE NEEDS A HAPPY ENDING

SAMMY AND THE PRINCESS, SCENE 26

INT. A TEEN CENTER IN SAMMY'S HOMETOWN—DAY

*KIDS PLAYING POOL, PING PONG, VIDEO GAMES,
ETC. CLARISSA AND SAMMY ENTER*

                    CLARISSA
Wow. This place is amazing.

                    SAMMY
Wow is definitely your favorite American word.

                    CLARISSA
It is a good word.

                    SAMMY
I guess it is.

          CLARISSA (Looking around)
Everyone seems so happy here.

                    SAMMY
Well, kids are happier when their
parents aren't around. It's been proven
in tests.

CLARISSA GIGGLES

                CLARISSA

I have had such a good time today,
visiting your town. Your parents are
so nice, and your house is lovely.

                SAMMY

Well, it's not exactly a castle fit for
a princess, but I'm glad you like it.

                CLARISSA

You don't need a castle to live a happy
life. You just need to love and be
loved.

                SAMMY

Stop being so smart. You're scaring me.

           CLARISSA (Giggling again)

Oh, Sammy. You make me laugh so much.
I've really enjoyed getting to know you
this year. What would I ever do without you?

                    SAMMY
      Um . . . hopefully suffer and be sad?

THEY LOOK AT EACH OTHER. SAMMY WONDERS—COULD
THIS PRINCESS ACTUALLY BE FALLING FOR HIM?

                    CLARISSA
      Come. Show me your favorite activity
      here.

HE STEERS HER OVER TO THE AIR HOCKEY TABLE

                    SAMMY
      This is my favorite game. It's called
      air hockey. You get to smash things,
      but nobody gets hurt.

THEY START PLAYING. SHE IS TERRIBLE, BUT SHE
SLOWLY GETS BETTER. FINALLY, SHE BEATS HIM.

                    CLARISSA
      I win! I win!

                    SAMMY
      But that's only because I've haven't
      eaten dinner yet. I'm feeling a little
      weak, I swear!

CLARISSA

Oh, Sammy, you are too much.

THEY LAUGH, AS A MIDDLE-SCHOOL-AGED BOY COMES
UP TO THEM

BOY

Hey, you're hogging the table. Give
someone else a chance.

SAMMY LOOKS AT THE KID LIKE HE'S ABOUT TO TELL
HIM TO BUZZ OFF. THEN CLARISSA TOUCHES SAMMY'S
ARM, AND HE MELTS LIKE A SNOWBALL ON A WARM
DAY.

SAMMY (To the kid)

Sure, it's all yours.

CLARISSA (To the kid)

We're sorry if we were preventing you
from playing. (To Sammy) What should
we do now?

SAMMY

(In a trance, still thinking about the
spot on his arm where Clarissa touched
him) Anything . . . As long as it's
with you . . .

                    CLARISSA (Confused)
          I'm sorry?

                    SAMMY (Snapping out of it)
          I mean . . . Anything! It's up to you.

                         CLARISSA
          You are a funny boy, Sammy Powell.

                         SAMMY
          I try. Believe me, I try.

SUDDENLY THERE'S A COMMOTION AT THE FRONT DOOR
OF THE TEEN CENTER. THEY LOOK TO SEE—IT'S
CROFT, ENTERING WITH SOME OF HIS BUDDIES.

                         SAMMY
          What the—?

CROFT AND HIS PALS COME OVER TO SAMMY AND
CLARISSA

                    SAMMY (Cont'd)
          What are you guys doing here?

CROFT

Yeah, the dance was boring, so I got
my dad's chauffeur to drive us down. I
wanted to see what a normal American
town was like, too!

(He looks at Clarissa)

Isn't that right, *Princess*?

CLARISSA (Shocked)

How did you find out?

CROFT'S FRIEND DARREN STEPS UP

DARREN

We've been wondering all year about
your accent, and your background, and
your weird name and everything. So
Croft asked me to ask my dad about
you, because my dad is on the Board of
Trustees, and they told him you were a
princess of some weird foreign country.

CLARISSA (Not able to hide
it any longer)

Yes. That is true.

SAMMY

So what? So what if she's a princess?

CROFT

Well, I'm thinking the princess might
want to take a ride in a limo.

SAMMY

She's with me.

CROFT LAUGHS

SAMMY (Cont'd)

What's that laugh supposed to mean?
That she can't be with someone like
me?

CROFT

That's exactly what it means. Let me
just give you a little piece of advice,
Sammy boy. Girls like Clarissa . . .
they don't end up with guys like you.
They end up with guys like *me*.

SAMMY LOOKS AT CLARISSA.

                        SAMMY
        Is that true?

SHE LOOKS DOWN . . .

                   CLARISSA (confused)
        I . . . I don't . . .

          SAMMY (Upset at her lack of support)
          Well, guess what, Princess? You're in
          luck, because I don't like you, either!

SAMMY AND CLARISSA STAND THERE FOR A SECOND,
NOT QUITE SURE WHAT TO DO NEXT.

                   CROFT (To Clarissa)
          So, yeah, like I said, we've got the
          limo outside. Come take a ride, we'll
          go back to the dance.

                        CLARISSA
          Why? So you can say you danced with a
          princess?

                         CROFT
          Nope. So I can say I *slow*-danced with
          a princess.

HE HIGH-FIVES HIS BUDDIES. CLARISSA IS UNEASY.

                    CLARISSA
          Croft, I am sorry, but I would prefer
          to stay here with my friend Sammy.

                      CROFT
          Seriously? You just said you didn't
          like him!

                    CLARISSA
          I never said that. *He* said that.

*SAMMY LOOKS AT CLARISSA. COULD SHE ACTUALLY
LIKE HIM?*

                      CROFT
          Yo, that is so lame! Don't you know
          who I am? My dad could buy and sell
          this town!

                    CLARISSA
          Croft, please—

*CROFT MOVES CLOSER TO HER, AND THINGS LOOK
LIKE THEY COULD GET WEIRD. SUDDENLY SAMMY RUNS
BETWEEN THEM.*

                    SAMMY

She said no!

                    CROFT

Are you serious?

               SAMMY (As nervous as he's
                 ever been in his life)
Clarissa wants to stay here and that's
final.

                    CROFT

Dude, stop pretending that you're her
boyfriend!

                    SAMMY

I'm way more than her boyfriend. I'm
her *best* friend.

*CLARISSA COMES OVER TO SAMMY AND STANDS BEHIND
HIM.*

                    DARREN

Yo, Croft, let's just get out of here
and get back to the dance.

*CROFT TAKES A LONG LOOK AT SAMMY AND CLARISSA,
THEN NODS.*

CROFT
Yeah, okay. Let's hit it.

THEY START TO LEAVE AND THEN CROFT TURNS BACK.

CROFT
Yo, Sammy!

*SAMMY BRACES FOR TROUBLE. BUT INSTEAD CROFT
SMACKS HIM AFFECTIONATELY ON THE SHOULDER.*

CROFT
You're a brave little dude. I respect
that.

HE AND HIS FRIENDS EXIT.

CLARISSA (To Sammy)
Thank you.

SAMMY LETS OUT THE LONGEST EXHALE EVER.

CLARISSA (Cont'd)

Are you okay?

                    SAMMY
Nothing that a heart transplant can't
fix.
    (After a few more deep breaths)
    So . . . did you want to finish your
sentence? "I don't . . ."

                   CLARISSA
I don't . . . want you to jump to any
conclusions.

                    SAMMY
Meaning . . . ?

                   CLARISSA
Oh, Sammy, let's not talk about it
anymore! I just want to have fun.

      SAMMY (Agreeing to move on)
Okay. Sounds good. Hey, have you ever
tried bumper pool?

SOMETIMES, EVEN SEVEN APOLOGIES AREN'T ENOUGH

I SPENT ALL WEEKEND AT HOME, trying to avoid everyone and everything. It worked, except for my parents and my sister, who treated me like I was the victim of a car accident, instead of a cake in the face.

By Saturday night, I couldn't take it any more. "Stop being so nice to me!" I yelled.

And they did.

Back at school on Monday, I kept to myself as much as possible.

I sat by myself at lunch, obviously.

That's right. The guy who, two months earlier, couldn't walk down the hall at school without getting bombarded by people wanting to be his best friend, sat there eating his fish sticks and drinking his chocolate milk completely alone. I decided to pass the time by making a few "tweaks" to the picture I drew of Shana, which I'd never ended up giving to her.

I changed it by adding a lot of pimples to her face.

Sometimes, pimples can really
make a guy feel better

The only sign at school that Friday night had even happened—that the Internet had been bombarded all weekend with pictures of Shana and me kissing, and me with cake up my nose—was in the cafeteria at lunch, where someone had erased OATMEAL COOKIES from the dessert blackboard and written CHOCOLATE CAKE WITH MILANO FROSTING.

Whoever said it's good to be the king?

To make things even more awkward, it was the day we were scheduled to shoot the scene at Jookie's, where

I'd gotten everyone parts as extras. And so, at exactly 1:00 p.m., I left class, as usual. But this time, all the other kids left class with me—Jake, Nareem, Katie, Eliza, Timmy, Hannah, and Charlie Joe. At first, it didn't look like Mareli was going to come after all, but at the last minute, I saw her come out of the library and join the rest of us.

"Cool, I wasn't sure you were coming," I told her. It was the eighth thing I'd said to her that day. The first seven were apologies.

I'm sorry. I'm sorry. I'm sorry. I'm sorry.
I'm sorry. I'm sorry. I'm sorry.
Cool, I wasn't sure you were coming.

It was like a small stampede as we left the school. Mrs. Sleep stood outside her office, staring at us with an annoyed expression on her face. She hadn't been all that thrilled when eight more kids told her that they needed to leave school early to be in the movie.

"What am I running here, a charm school?" she'd thundered. I wasn't sure what a charm school was, but it sounded kind of fun.

In the school parking lot there was a giant van waiting, instead of my usual car. But most kids drove with their parents, since Jookie's was only ten minutes away. The only people who got into the van besides me were Charlie Joe, Katie, and Timmy.

Ashley was there, too, of course.

"So, you guys must be the friends Pete wanted so desperately to get into the movie," she said. "The ones who then embarrassed the heck out of him last night, in front of about a zillion photographers." Ashley had grown a little protective of me. I kind of liked it.

"Hey, we didn't tell Pete to kiss Shana Fox right in front of his girlfriend," Charlie Joe said. He always liked to get right to the point.

"I still can't believe Mareli smushed cake in my face," I said.

"You know what?" said Charlie Joe. "It reminded me of something *you* would do. In the old days, at least."

I looked at him. "What do you mean by that?"

Katie said, "He means, you used to be a little crazy. Okay, a *lot* crazy."

"Exactly," Charlie Joe added. "But now, you're just . . . I don't know . . . too cool for school sometimes."

"I am not!" I protested. "I'm still crazy."

"Whatever," said Charlie Joe. "I miss the old you."

"*We* miss the old you," added Timmy.

"It's not that simple, you guys," I said. "It's more complicated than that."

"It always is," added Katie.

Ashley, who'd been listening to this whole thing, let out a big sigh. "Well, at least it's a story you all can tell your grandkids."

"And I vote none of us talk about it until then," I said, hoping to put an end to that topic of conversation. And it worked. But it worked a little too well.

It put an end to *all* conversation.

JOOKIE'S

WHEN WE GOT TO JOOKIE'S, the first thing I saw was Sheldon Felden on the front lawn, hitting golf balls into a little cup.

"Hey, kid," he said, not looking up. "You got your pals with you?"

I hesitated. The last thing I wanted was to get in a whole long conversation about how my friends had let me down. Or vice versa.

"Don't worry, kid, I'm not gonna give you the third degree," Mr. Felden said, reading my mind. "Just tell them not to look at the camera. First rule of being an extra. Never look at the camera!"

"Yes, sir. I mean, Mr. Felden."

"Don't call me Mr. Felden, either!" he barked. "It makes me feel old. Or, I should say, it reminds me that I *am* old." He handed his golf club to an assistant, while another assistant brought him a Fresca. (Have you ever seen anyone under sixty-five drink a Fresca? Me neither.) "Hollywood is a young person's game, Pete. Because only young people can handle the crazy stuff that happens in this business."

He and I both knew exactly what he was referring to.

He took a big swig of his drink. "I don't know if you noticed, but I'm not young anymore. But you are. And you're a good kid. You can handle it, I'm not worried."

I wish everyone in the movie business were as cool as Sheldon Felden.

* * *

Jookie's was the social center for kids in our town. It had pool tables, Ping-Pong, video games, and the best milkshakes in town. There was a stage, too, where bands sometimes played (Katie Friedman's band, CHICKMATE, played there once and blew the doors off). The place was pretty popular, although not very big—it could only hold about a hundred kids.

But that day, there had to be a thousand people crammed in there.

It was as if the entire movie studio had moved to Jookie's—including all the people with headsets running around, and the wires, and the food tables, and the giant lights.

My friends from school looked like they were sleep-walking through a dream. Which they were, kind of.

"This is crazy," murmured Charlie Joe.

The rest of them nodded in agreement.

I introduced everyone to a few of the guys on the crew and showed them the craft services table (they were in awe), then we heard someone yell, "Hey!" Will, the long-haired guy from my audition, was running over to us at a full sprint. "Okay, kids, come with me!"

We all started to follow him into the main auditorium, but he stopped me. "Not you, Pete. The stars are using the mobile homes outside."

" 'Stars?' " Katie said, rolling her eyes.

Oh, boy, here we go.

The scenes we were shoot-ing in Eastport were about the day Sammy takes Clarissa to his home-town and shows her around, since she wants to see how regular Ameri-cans really live. They visit the ice cream parlor, the beach, and wind up at a place a lot like Jookie's, where Clarissa tries air hockey for the very first time.

When you shoot on location, it's different. For one thing, there isn't a lot of room for things like dressing rooms and stuff, so they rent these giant mobile homes where the actors get ready. Main Street in Eastport was filled with so many trailers, it looked like an invasion from outer space. Not to mention the fact that the police had the whole street blocked off.

"Pete!"

I turned to see Shana getting out of her limo, accompanied by the usual five people that went everywhere with her, plus Bear the Chihuahua.

She came over to give me a big hug and kiss. "Did you and Mareli make up? I feel so bad about what happened. The websites went crazy!"

"They sure did," I said.

"Well, I am going to be super nice to her today!"

"Do you think you can tell her that we're not really boyfriend and girlfriend?"

Shana looked pained. "Oh, Pete, you know I would if I could. But I think we should just let the story build for a while. It will be so great for the movie!"

"Build, like, for how long?" I asked.

"I don't *know*," Shana said impatiently. "Stop bugging me about it. Ask Iris, it was her idea in the first place."

Iris!?!? I couldn't believe it. "What? Are you kidding me?"

"Yeah I know. She's kind of a genius that way." Shana took out a tiny mirror and started examining her face. "When are you going to introduce me to your friends properly?"

I shook my head. "I'm not sure that's a good idea."

"Come on!" Shana put her sunglasses on. "I need to make sure they don't hate me! Let's do it before I go into makeup."

I looked at Ashley, who glanced at her watch and sighed. By then, even I knew the first rule of show business: The star gets to do whatever she wants.

We headed inside and found my friends sitting around, waiting to be told what to do.

"What's taking so long?" I heard Jake's mom complain to a random crew guy. "These children are just wasting time, doing nothing!"

The crew guy just shrugged.

"Sorry, Mrs. Katz," I told her. "Everything takes a long time in the movie business. There's a lot of waiting."

She raised her eyebrows. "Oh, so you're an expert now? Very nice."

"Some guy said they were going to come and take our measurements for clothes," Hannah said. "But he walked away and we haven't seen him since."

"I'll try to find out what's going on," Ashley told them.

Then, as if a lightbulb were switched on, everyone noticed Shana.

"Whoa," said Timmy.

"Hey," said Charlie Joe.

"I just wanted to welcome everyone to the set!" Shana chirped.

Everyone stared with their mouths open. Even the parents.

"Last night was crazy, huh?" said Shana. When no one answered her, she added, "I hope everybody has a great day!"

I heard a few gulps and gurgles from my friends, but no actual words.

"Anyway, I just love Pete," Shana went on. "I have to tell you, he's been so great to work with. A real professional."

"A real professional?" said Charlie Joe. "Pete Milano? Are we talking about the same guy?"

"Yup! He's awesome!" added Shana. I think she was trying to help. But judging by the looks I was getting from my friends, she wasn't.

"She doesn't mean it," I said. "She's just being nice."

"I am not!" she said, smacking me. Then Shana spotted Mareli, and she put on her concerned face. "Hi again. You must be Mareli. Pete's told me so much about you. I just want to make sure you're not mad at me for last night. It was all a terrible misunderstanding."

I looked at Mareli, waiting to see what she would do. After a few seconds, she came forward. "Hello," she said.

They shook hands. "You really are so pretty," Shana said. "And I love those earrings!"

Mareli tried not to look flattered. "Thank you. I made them."

"You made them?" Shana's eyes went wide. "That's amazing! Can you make me, like, twenty pairs, in various colors?"

Mareli's eyes went wide. "Twenty pairs? Seriously?"

"Totally seriously!" Shana looked at Ashley. "Hon, can you have Bernie write Mareli a check? That'd be great." She looked back at Mareli. "Bernie does my money. Just let him know how much it will be."

"You mean you'll pay me?"

"Of course!"

A woman who had about fourteen rips in her jeans came up to Shana and whispered in her ear. "Well, see you guys later," Shana said. "Gotta run." And she was off.

Everyone watched her go, as if they were watching the President of the United States drive by.

"She's really pretty," Timmy said. "Like, really, really pretty."

"I still can't believe you know her," Hannah said. "And I especially can't believe you kissed her."

But instead of answering them, I ran after Shana.

"What was that about?" I asked her.

She kept walking. "What was what?"

"Asking Mareli to make you twenty pairs of earrings? And saying you'll pay her for them?"

Shana whirled on me. "What's your problem? I told you I wanted to be extra nice to her!"

"You were showing off," I said. "Showing off in front of my girlfriend. My real girlfriend! As opposed to you, my fake girlfriend."

"Whatever," Shana said. "I don't have time for this."

"You probably don't even like her earrings."

"You're probably right."

And she walked away, leaving me—as usual—halfway between my movie star life and my friends from home.

QUITE A SCENE

IT GOT WORSE FROM THERE.

The kids from school waited for two more hours while Shana and I shot some close-up dialogue. They weren't even allowed to watch because it was a closed set—meaning, no outsiders.

Then, finally, we were ready to shoot the crowd scene.

"Okay, Pete's pals, let's do this!" Will yelled. By then, they were crashing from all the chocolate chip cookies and soda they'd scarfed down. But they dragged themselves over to the set.

"In this scene, Sammy is teaching Clarissa how to play air hockey," Will explained. "You guys are going to be playing other various games in the background. At one point, one of you will come over and say, 'Hey, you're hogging the table.' Who wants to do that?"

Charlie Joe, Eliza, and Timmy raised their hands.

"Okay, let me hear you each say it," the guy said.

"Hey, you're hogging the table," Eliza said.

"Hey, you're hogging the table," Timmy said.

"Hey, you're hogging the table," Charlie Joe said.

The clipboard guy thought for a minute, then pointed at Charlie Joe. "You," he said.

"So what do the rest of us do?" asked Katie.

"Not much, apparently," answered Jake.

"Will they even see our faces?" asked Timmy.

"Most definitely not," answered Nareem.

"This stinks," concluded Eliza.

But wait, there's more.

After we shot the scene the first time, Nano, who hadn't even introduced himself to anyone, came over. "The shot is too crowded," he announced. Then he pointed at Katie and Jake. "You two, please step out."

"Step out?" asked Katie.

Nano didn't answer, but his assistant gently guided the two of them back to the crafts services table.

The second time we shot the scene, Shana stopped in the middle. "I'm sorry, but something is distracting me," she said. "I think maybe the light is bouncing off somebody's earrings?"

"Nope, no shadows," said the lighting guy.

Nano pointed at Mareli. "Let's lose the earrings," he said.

In the middle of the third take, Shana stopped again. This time she looked directly at Mareli. "Do you mind if I ask why you're moving your arms so much?"

"I'm playing Ping-Pong," Mareli said.

"Can we have Mareli do something other than play Ping-Pong?" Shana asked-slash-demanded. "She's making these big sweeping motions with her arms and I can see it out of the corner of my eye. It's distracting."

Nano gave an impatient groan. "Can someone please have this young lady stand over by the soda machine?"

But Mareli wasn't interested in standing by the soda machine. In fact, she wasn't interested in standing anywhere. Instead, she came over to the air hockey table and parked herself right between Shana and me.

"I don't think I want to be in this movie anymore," she announced. Then she turned around and looked at Shana. "And I will not make you earrings for all the money in the world."

This can't be good.

As Mareli marched off the set, I felt my heart pounding. I looked around, not sure what would happen next. I caught Jake's eye, and he whispered something to me, but I couldn't quite hear what he said. I leaned closer, and he repeated it.

"Do something," he said.

"Huh?"

"Do something," he repeated.

And I understood.

"Wait!" I yelled. "Mareli, wait!"

Mareli stopped. "Now what? Another worthless apology?"

I ran over to her.

"Pete!" Nano barked. "Get back on set—we need to shoot!"

"Hold on," I barked back at him. That got everyone's attention. People on movie sets generally didn't speak to directors like that. Even lousy directors.

"I want to leave," Mareli told me.

"I know you do," I said, "and I don't blame you. But just let me say one last thing. I don't like Shana. I really don't. Maybe I was confused, because it's confusing when a world-famous star acts like they like you, but I know the truth now. I like you."

Mareli looked at me like she was trying to decide whether or not to believe me.

"Remember that dinner at my house?" I went on, "You

kind of made it seem like you didn't want to go out with me anymore anyway."

"That's not what I said," Mareli insisted. Then she glanced over at Shana. "So she doesn't like you?"

"Nope," I said. "She's just pretending that I'm her boyfriend so people will write about us as a couple to help the movie and make her real boyfriend jealous. That's what people do in the movie business. They pretend."

I suddenly realized how quiet it was, because everyone had stopped working so they could listen. Even the crew guys. And they don't care about *anything*.

Mareli walked back over to Shana. "Is that true?" she asked.

"All I know," Shana said, "is that usually when I kiss a boy, they look like they've just hit a home run to win the World Series. But not Pete." She looked at me. "Pete looked like he struck out." Shana smiled, and for a second she actually looked like any other fifteen-year-old girl. "Pete's all yours," she said to Mareli. "You're the one he likes."

I was pretty sure the home run line was from some other movie Shana was in, but I wasn't about to tell Mareli that. Especially since she turned around and gave me a giant hug.

"I'm sorry I threw a cake in your face," Mareli said.

"That's okay," I answered. "It was delicious."

We both laughed. It was the best I'd felt in a long time. And it lasted about six seconds.

Which is when I felt a sharp tap on my shoulder.

I turned around and saw Nano standing there, twirling his obnoxious scarf.

"Hey, Nano," I said. "Just give us a second."

"Oh, I'll give you more than a second!" he thundered. "I'll give you the rest of your life!"

I looked at him. "What does that mean?"

He started pacing back and forth. "It means that this whole thing was a mistake. Auditioning you was a mistake, but I let Iris talk me into it. Casting you was a mistake, but I let Sheldon talk me into it. And letting your friends be extras and disrupt my set was the biggest mistake of all—and I don't even know WHO talked me into that one! So either you end this little middle school drama right now and get back to work, or we can escort you right out of here, with the rest of your pals—because their short little movie careers are OVER!"

No one moved. The only sound you could hear was the

buzzing of the fans that were used to keep all the equipment cool.

Then, finally, someone spoke. It was Charlie Joe.

"Who IS this guy?" he said.

Ashley walked over, trying to calm things down. "Everything is fine, Nano," she said. "You don't need to speak to Pete that way. If anyone caused this drama, it was Shana. Pete's doing a great job on the movie; Mr. Felden is very pleased with his performance. So let's just forget the whole thing and get back to work."

"What do you know?" Nano told Ashley. "You're just a babysitter."

"How dare you," Ashley hissed at him.

Nano shrugged. "We can forget it, as long as someone gets all these annoying kids out of here." He turned to his assistant. "Get me some new extras up from the city, right away."

Everyone slowly started going about their business, and it seemed like the craziness was over. Except for one person. One person was not quite ready to forget it.

Me.

I marched over to Nano. "Thank you for giving me the choice of either going back to work, or leaving with my friends," I said. "I've thought it over, and I'm going to leave with my friends."

I started to walk away, but then I turned back. "Oh, I

almost forgot something." I pointed at his big red scarf.
"I've always really, really hated that thing."

Then I grabbed the scarf, hugged Mareli, and ran.

Nano screamed bloody murder and threw in a few
swear words for good measure. Then he bellowed, "STOP
THAT LITTLE TWERP!"—which, by the way, is exactly
what Mrs. Collins called me when I took her daughter's
pom-poms.

But I was too fast for all of them.

The last thing I saw as I sprinted out of Jookie's was
Sheldon Felden.

He was laughing his head off.

Old habits die hard, as it turns out.

ON THE RUN AGAIN

SO, THERE I WAS AGAIN, running away after taking something I shouldn't have taken.

But this time, I knew exactly where I was going, and I didn't have a furious mother chasing me. Just a bunch of out-of-shape union guys.

I turned right out of Jookie's, sprinted down Pine Street, looped around the little league fields, and hooked a left down Harding Lane toward downtown.

By the time I got to Just Brew It, I was out of breath in that *uh-oh, I'm in trouble* kind of way. It reminded me of the old days.

Which is probably why it felt great.

The tattooed guy with all the piercings was there, right where I'd left him. He gave me a little wave. Then I turned around, and sure enough, there she was—sitting in the same exact spot I'd seen her when I first met her, what seemed like a lifetime ago.

"Hey, Iris."

It's déjà vu all over again.

She didn't seem surprised to see me. "Hey."

"How come you're not at the set?" I asked.

"I'd just get in the way."

"Oh."

After a minute, I decided to bring it up.

"So, um . . . why did you tell Shana to kiss me in the restaurant?"

Iris closed her computers and looked at me. "Because I'm in the movie business, and I do whatever it takes to make sure my movies are successful. And lots of attention helps make a movie successful."

I shook my head. "But you had to know what would happen."

"And what happened?" she said, smiling. "You stood up for yourself, and everyone lived happily ever after."

"Not necessarily," I said. "Nano is about to kill me."

She took a sip of her drink. "Well, it just so happens I have news about that as well."

"You do?"

"Yeah, isn't technology amazing? Have a seat, while I help sort this thing out."

I did.

We sat there quietly, as I caught my breath. Watching her work was like watching someone with four hands. Finally, she looked up from her phone and chuckled.

"Well, that's that. Sheldon just fired Nano."

I wasn't sure I heard her correctly. "What?"

"Yup," Iris said.

"Jeez."

"Don't feel guilty," she said, reading my mind. "I'm only surprised it took this long."

She got up, gathered all her stuff, went outside, and got into a car. Somehow, I knew to follow her and get in, too.

"Guess who's taking over?" Iris asked.

"I have no idea."

She told the driver to take us to Jookie's, then looked at me and smiled.

"Ashley," she said.

BACK TO SCHOOL

AFTER NANO GOT FIRED and Ashley took over, the rest of the shooting went really well. Everything got back to normal—well, as normal as things can get when you're shooting a movie.

Sammy and the Princess comes out next summer. The premiere is in New York City at the Ziegfeld Theatre on July 20. My whole family is going to come, and a ton of my friends. My girlfriend Mareli will be there, too. Afterward, there is going to be a big party catered by my dad, because Shana Fox really loves his pizza.

I'm a little worried about the reaction. What if people think I'm a bad actor? Shana said most actors don't read their reviews—but I'm pretty sure I'm not going to be able to help it. But maybe it won't be so bad. There have already been some blog posts by people who somehow have seen parts of the movie or something, although I don't know how that happens. My favorite was on the website TeenMovie.com, which said, "Pete Milano looks like someone to keep an eye on—he's adorable and funny, and seems like a kid we'd like to hang around with." That made me feel good, because it was written by kids.

So that's about it for my experience making a movie. It was really fun, even though it got a little crazy there for a while. I recommend it to everyone, if they have the chance, but I know that's not likely. I know how lucky I was. And I'll never forget it.

I stopped reading. Then I looked up at Mrs. Sleep, Ms. Ferrell, and Mrs. Albone, who were all sitting in front of me.

... and that's how I became a famous movie star

"Very nice job," said Mrs. Sleep. "I'm glad you took this assignment seriously, Mr. Milano. Your paper was very thoughtful and well written."

"I agree," said Ms. Ferrell. "Well done, Pete."

Mrs. Albone nodded. "Well done indeed," she said. Then she smiled. "Maybe you should make a movie more often."

Everyone laughed except Mrs. Sleep. "Mrs. Albone brings up a good point, Peter," she said. "Now that it's over, how do you feel about the experience? Is it something you want to continue doing?"

"Wow," I said. "I'm not sure. I hadn't really thought about it."

Mrs. Sleep pushed her glasses up on her nose. "Well, you may have to think about it, especially if others agree with the people on that website."

I thought for a second. I knew Sheldon Felden liked me—after we'd finished shooting, he'd pulled me aside and said, "Kid. I think you got it. And there are people out there who are going to want it." So maybe that means I would get an offer to act in another movie. And that would mean more excitement, more people thinking I was talented, more cool people to meet, and more getting to pretend I was someone else. But it would also mean more drama at school, and more jealousy and stuff with my friends, and more missed soccer games. And also, aren't there a ton of young people who act in movies and get all conceited and think they're awesome, and then when they become adults their careers are over, because they're not cute kids anymore? Who needs that???

"So, what's it going to be, Pete?" Ms. Ferrell asked. "Do you want to be an actor, or do you want to have a normal life?"

I thought for a second.

"Yes," I said.

* * *

When I got outside Mrs. Sleep's office, all my friends were waiting for me.

"How'd it go?" asked Charlie Joe.

I waited a beat (dramatic pause), then gave the thumbs-up.

"I will live to see another day," I said.

I high-fived Timmy, Charlie Joe, and Katie. Then I grabbed Mareli's hand, pulled her toward me, and kissed her—right on the lips.

"I owed you that," I told her.

"Payment accepted," she told me.

Everyone hooted and hollered.

It was just like in a movie.

SAMMY AND THE PRINCESS, FINAL SCENE

EXT. OUTSIDE THE DORM—DAY

IT'S THE LAST DAY OF THE YEAR—PARENTS PICKING UP THEIR KIDS. SAMMY'S MOM AND DAD ARE HELPING HIM LOAD UP THE CAR.

> DAD
>
> So, quite a year, huh son?

> SAMMY
>
> That's one way to put it, yeah.

> MOM
>
> I don't know what it is about you, Sammy, but . . . you've changed. You've grown up.

> SAMMY
>
> Is that a good thing?

> MOM
>
> It's a very good thing.

CROFT COMES UP TO THE CAR.

CROFT

See you around, little man.

THEY FIST BUMP.

SAMMY

Mom, Dad, you remember Croft.

THEY DON'T LOOK TOO THRILLED TO SEE HIM.

SAMMY (Cont'd)

Don't worry, you guys. We're pals now.
We respect each other.

CROFT

That's right, Mr. and Mrs. Powell. Your
son . . . he stands up for what he
believes in. That's pretty cool. See
you around, bro!

*HE PUNCHES SAMMY ON THE ARM. SAMMY WINCES,
THEN PUNCHES CROFT BACK—A SAD, LITTLE PUNCH.*

CROFT

Dude, you gotta start lifting.

                    SAMMY
        I'll get right on that.

CROFT WAVES AND WALKS AWAY.

                    MOM
        So, where's . . .

                    SAMMY
        Clarissa?

                    MOM
        Yes, Clarissa. If you don't mind my
        asking.

                    DAD
        She's a terrific girl.

                    SAMMY
        She's . . . with her parents, I think.
        There's probably a ton of security
        around them and stuff. I'll just send
        her a text or something.

THEY'RE JUST ABOUT TO DRIVE AWAY WHEN . . .

                        CLARISSA
Sammy! Sammy, wait!

CLARISSA COMES RUNNING UP.

                        CLARISSA
I just wanted you to know . . . that
you're the best friend I've ever had.

                        SAMMY
I am?

                        CLARISSA
Yes. And one day . . . I know you will
make a princess very, very happy.

THEY LOOK AT EACH OTHER FOR A LONG MOMENT.

                        SAMMY
Any princess in particular?

                    CLARISSA (After a pause)
Perhaps.

THEY HUG. THEN SAMMY GETS IN HIS CAR AND THEY
DRIVE AWAY. SAMMY SITS IN THE BACK, LOOKING
OUT THE WINDOW AND THINKING.

                    DAD
So Sammy, overall . . . if you had to
pick one thing . . . what would be the
most important thing you learned this
year?

A LONG PAUSE BEFORE SAMMY FINALLY ANSWERS.

                   SAMMY
Life can be really weird sometimes.

                    MOM
Oh, come on! You can do better than that!

                   SAMMY
Okay, okay, fine! (He thinks)
   Life can be really weird some-
times . . .
   So through it all, you need to remem-
ber to hold on to what's more important.
   (He thinks some more)
   And never teach air hockey to a
princess on an empty stomach.

AND THEY DRIVE OFF INTO THE DISTANCE.

FADE TO BLACK . . .

                  THE END

CLOSING CREDITS

Pete Milano took all his friends to the world premiere of the movie, which was held at Jookie's in Eastport. Afterward, there was an air-hockey tournament; Jake Katz came in first, shocking everyone.

Sammy and the Princess went on to become a big hit, with reviewers praising the film's "authentic feel" and "plausible storyline."

Mareli Quinones made Pete another chocolate/coconut cake—this time for the premiere—and it turned out to be even more delicious when it was served on plates.

Pete and Shana Fox signed on to star in the sequel, *Sammy and the Princess: Malvanian Summer!*—to be directed by **Ashley Kinsley**.

Dex Bannion declined to be a part of the film, because he was on tour with his band, THE DOG WOOFERS.

Sheldon Felden celebrated the success of the movie by marrying his longtime girlfriend, twenty-seven-year-old actress/waitress Misty Plains.

Nano—whose real name turned out to be Seymour Wiffler—decided to quit directing and become a full-time knitter. He specializes in scarves.